GIRLS'
Weekend in
VEGAS

Four friends, four dream weddings!

On a girly weekend in Las Vegas, best friends
Alex, Molly, Serena and Jayne are supposed to
just have fun and forget men—but they end up
meeting their perfect matches! Will the love
they find in Vegas stay in Vegas?

Find out in this sassy, fun and wildly romantic
miniseries all about love and friendship.

This month meet Serena
Inconveniently Wed! by Jackie Braun

Next month meet Jayne
Wedding Date with the Best Man by Melissa McClone

Dear Reader,

Writing is usually a very solitary profession, so I jumped at the chance to be part of the GIRLS' WEEKEND IN VEGAS continuity series with fellow authors Myrna Mackenzie, Shirley Jump and Melissa McClone.

We put our heads together, electronically speaking, for several weeks to come up with the overall concept. Then, as we wrote our individual books, we kept in touch via e-mail to exchange information on our characters and to share how our stories were— or in some cases, were not—coming along.

At times I found it difficult to keep our timelines straight and the details clear as our stories intersected and our characters interacted. But I wouldn't have missed it for the world. In a way, the four of us had our own girls' weekend in Vegas— though it lasted a bit longer than that, involved more work than play, and we never got to set foot on the Strip.

I hope you enjoy Serena and Jonas's story—and don't forget to pick up Melissa McClone's book next month to find out how the series ends!

Best wishes,

Jackie Braun

JACKIE BRAUN

Inconveniently Wed!

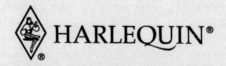

TORONTO • NEW YORK • LONDON
AMSTERDAM • PARIS • SYDNEY • HAMBURG
STOCKHOLM • ATHENS • TOKYO • MILAN • MADRID
PRAGUE • WARSAW • BUDAPEST • AUCKLAND

Recycling programs
for this product may
not exist in your area.

ISBN-13: 978-0-373-74046-8

INCONVENIENTLY WED!

First North American Publication 2010.

This edition published by arrangement with Harlequin Books S.A.

For questions and comments about the quality of this book please contact us at Customer_eCare@Harlequin.ca.

www.eHarlequin.com

Printed in U.S.A.

Jackie Braun is a three-time RITA® Award finalist, a four-time National Readers' Choice Award finalist and a past winner of the Rising Star Award. She worked for nearly two decades as an award-winning journalist before leaving her full-time job to write fiction. She lives in mid-Michigan with her husband and their two sons. She loves to hear from readers and can be reached through her Web site at www.jackiebraun.com.

My thanks to Melissa, Shirley and Myrna
for including me in the fun.

CHAPTER ONE

FOR a woman like Serena Warren, Las Vegas was heaven. Everything about the place was outrageous and over the top—just like she was. Too bad she was only there for the weekend. She'd come on a sisterhood mission of sorts, with her three friends—Molly Hunter, Alexandra Lowell and Jayne Cavendish—after Jayne's fiancé had turned out to be a lying, cheating, son of a…jerk.

They'd kicked up their high heels on Friday night and most of Saturday. Even Jayne had managed to have some fun. She'd gone to a salon and had her trademark long locks snipped off into an adorable short do that would have left her ex suitably appalled. But as Saturday wound down, so did Jayne.

Even though the friends had planned a second storming of the Strip, Jayne decided to spend the evening in the hotel's spa and pool complex. And Alex, her roommate for the evening, had opted to stay with her—not only to keep Jayne company, but because she had a lot of thinking to do herself. The owner of McKendrick's, the resort where they were staying, had offered Alex a job. It was an incredible opportunity, but if she took it not only would she have to move to Las Vegas, she would have to stay behind when the others returned to San Diego the following day.

"Tear up the Strip on our behalf," Alex instructed after Molly and Serena had offered to share some spa time, too.

"Are you sure?" Molly asked.

"Positive," Jayne said. "There's no reason the two of you shouldn't go out and have a good time."

The smile Jayne offered was genuine, even if it didn't quite reach her eyes. None of her smiles did these days.

"All right. If you insist." Serena grinned wickedly. "Las Vegas won't know what hit it when we're through."

"Dear God, what have we done?" Alex muttered in mock dismay. "This town will never be the same."

Jayne was more circumspect. "Try not to do anything too crazy. Especially you, Serena."

Serena blinked innocently and held up two fingers. "Scouts' honor. I won't do anything you wouldn't do."

Her quasi-promise was already forgotten an hour later, as she and Molly stood on the patio of one of the Bellagio's crowded lounges, watching its famed fountains as they waited for a table to open up.

"I wonder if I'd get arrested for dancing under the spray," she mused aloud.

Molly was used to her friend's antics and merely rolled her eyes. "Let's not find out, okay?"

"I'm not saying I plan to do it." Serena lifted her shoulders. "Just wondering, that's all."

"I wish Alex and Jayne had come out with us."

"I know. Do you think Jayne's having a good time?" Serena asked.

"About as good as she can under the circumstances."

"If I ever get my hands on that—"

"She's better off without him," Molly interjected.

"That goes without saying, but I hate that Rich walked away unscathed after all the pain and humiliation he caused her."

"He'll get his eventually," Molly predicted.

"I want to be there when he does. Maybe even help the process along a little, you know?"

"I do, indeed. Men can be such idiots." Molly's tone turned wistful then. "Still, they do have their uses."

"And some of them aren't hard to look at either," Serena added as she caught a glimpse of a blond-haired god of a man.

Gorgeous was an understatement. Something about him, something more than his looks, had her heart ticking out an extra beat. Before she could figure out what it was, though, he was swallowed up by the crowd.

The first thing Jonas Benjamin noticed as he walked through the Bellagio's bustling lounge was the redhead standing at the patio rail. She was impossible to miss—and not only because of the neon colors in her tie-dyed cropped jacket.

She had her back to him, so he couldn't see her face, but talk about a killer pair of legs. Slender, yet shapely, they gave the illusion of going on forever thanks to the skinny jeans that hugged her curves from thigh to ankle. They ended just shy of dagger-like leopard-print heels.

As water shot high into the air behind her she turned, and Jonas glimpsed her face. Her features were as stunning as he'd anticipated: high cheekbones, lushly fringed eyes, a slightly upturned nose beneath which a pair of pouting lips were slicked with red gloss. Lust wasn't unexpected, but the powerful zap of recognition he experienced was.

It made no sense. He didn't know the woman. He'd never seen her before and wasn't likely to again, since most if not all the bar's patrons were tourists. Added to that, she wasn't his type. Too unconventional, and way too flashy. His gaze skimmed her colorful jacket before focusing on a pair of earrings that dangled practically to her shoulders. The women he dated dressed conservatively. When it came to jewelry they leaned toward pearl studs or gold posts. They wouldn't be caught dead in quarter-sized hoops, let alone silver chandeliers that dripped with iridescent beads. The redhead's slightest movement caused the earrings to sway. The effect was mesmerizing, almost hypnotic.

Jonas rubbed his eyes and dismissed the bizarre feeling that he'd somehow been waiting for her. He was overworked, and with his campaign for mayor heading toward the final stretch had gone far too long without intimate female companionship. It was eleven o'clock on a Saturday night and he'd just come from a meeting with his campaign manager, Jameson Culver. They'd spent the better part of five hours discussing how best to capitalize on Jonas's most recent poll numbers, which showed him slightly ahead of his opponent.

It was no small coup that a political novice such as Jonas had managed to snag the veteran strategist for his camp. Still, Jameson was tedious and humorless. If possible he could be even more overbearing than Jonas's father, Corbin Benjamin, who'd enjoyed two terms as Nevada's governor in the 1990s before being elected to Congress, where he still served.

"You'll need more than a stint on the city's planning board on your political résumé if you expect to someday lead the State or move on to Washington," Corbin liked to remind him. "Mayor will be a good start."

A good start and a good ending. Jonas felt he had a lot to offer as Las Vegas's mayor, but he didn't have the stomach for state or national politics—not that he'd ever been able to convince his father of that.

He tugged at his necktie. God, he needed a drink. It was why he'd come. He knew he could relax in obscurity amid the tourists. Not many locals patronized the place unless they were entertaining out-of-town guests. From the corner of his eye he saw a couple leave. He headed to their table, arriving at the same time as the redhead, who had an attractive brunette in tow.

"I'll flip you for it," she said.

Given her looks, he had expected her voice to be husky. It was smooth as velvet.

"I've got a better idea. How about we share it?" Even as Jonas struggled to process the fact that he'd just made that suggestion, he was making another. "I'll even buy you and your friend a drink."

"I don't know." She tilted her head to one side, considering. The earrings undulated and his pulse picked up speed. "I'm not sure if you'll care for our conversation."

"I've got a sister." Jonas shrugged. "I think I can handle a bit of girl talk if it means I get to sit down." Who knew when the next table would become available? Surely that was the only reason he'd offered to share it in the first place?

The redhead laughed. The sound was rich and robust, just as he'd anticipated. What he wasn't prepared for was the way her sultry features took on an engagingly impish quality. Just that fast she went from searing siren to gamine girl-next-door. It was quite a transformation, and even though Jonas hadn't a clue as to what had inspired her mirth, he found himself grinning back and wanting to find out.

"What's so amusing?"

"Trust me, you don't want to know," the brunette murmured.

"Come on," Jonas coaxed.

The redhead shrugged. "Okay, but don't say you weren't warned. My friend and I were just discussing the most painful way to castrate a man."

Jonas winced, and resisted the urge to lower his hands in a protective gesture. "You're talking figuratively, right?"

A pair of red lips curved in answer.

"Ok*aaay,*" he said slowly. "Any man in particular, or the whole of the species?"

The redhead laughed. "Don't worry, Adonis. Your goods are safe." Just as he started to relax, though, she added, "For now," and laughed again.

"Do you still want to share a table with

us?" the brunette asked. She was doing her best to hide a grin.

"Why not? I like to live dangerously."

"Yeah, you look it," the redhead remarked as her gaze skimmed from his necktie to his wingtips.

"Appearances can be deceiving," he replied. She sobered at that, as if his words struck a chord. He stuck out a hand. "I'm Jonas."

"Serena."

Interesting name. As far as he could tell the woman was walking chaos. So far nothing about her could be considered serene, and that included her handshake. Sexual awareness surged through him the moment their palms pressed together. Her eyes rounded and she tugged her hand free. Jonas wasn't sure knowing she'd felt it too made him feel the least bit better.

She motioned toward her friend. "This is…um…"

"Molly," the brunette supplied, appearing more amused than insulted by her friend's sudden lapse in memory.

"It's nice to meet you, Molly."

He shook the young woman's hand. No shock of electricity accompanied the contact. Jonas almost wished it had. With her tidy appearance, she was far more his type. They took their seats as a busboy arrived to remove the cocktail glasses left by the previous occupants.

"So, how are you ladies enjoying your stay at the Bellagio?" he asked.

"Actually, we're guests at McKendrick's," Molly corrected.

"How did you know we were tourists?" Serena asked.

"Just a hunch." Though he was oddly tempted to give her earring a flick, he signaled for a server instead.

"I'm guessing you're here for a convention." Serena didn't keep *her* hands to herself. She reached for his tie and gave it a little tug, before allowing the length of silk to spill through her fingers. "Accountant?"

"Close."

"Yeah?"

"No." He smiled up at the young woman who'd come to take their order. "I'd like a bourbon neat, please."

"A vodka martini. Make it dirty," Serena added.

Jonas had to bite back a groan.

"Just ice water for me," Molly said.

"Are you sure?" he asked. "Remember, I'm buying."

"Thanks, but I feel a headache coming on." She massaged one temple.

"Vegas can do that," he commiserated. "You have to pace yourself."

"Where's the fun in that?" Serena wanted to know. "You've loosened your tie, Adonis, but I'm betting you never really let loose."

"Ah, ah, ah. Appearances, remember?" God, he was enjoying himself.

"What was the last crazy thing you did?"

"The last crazy thing?"

"Yeah." She tilted her head again and the earrings danced.

He reached over and flicked the ends of one.

Serena laughed outright. "Is that the best you can do?"

Jonas had thought it pretty major. He wasn't big on spontaneity. He usually thought things through, carefully weighing the risks and benefits, before acting or making a decision. Doing so served him well in his profession. In addition to running for mayor, he was a contract lawyer. As such, he paid close attention to the fine print—and to the effect it could have on one's life or livelihood.

"I'm waiting, Adonis." Her smile was smug.

His gaze lingered on her lips. They looked soft and sweet and way too inviting. Crazy?

What he was thinking of doing right now certainly qualified. He waited for sanity to return. It didn't, and instead of stepping back from the ledge he jumped off it.

"How about this?" he asked as he cupped the back of Serena's neck and pulled her toward him.

The kiss was brief and, as public displays of affection went, hardly over the top. Yet it proved to be as big a turn-on as foreplay. Even the zap of electricity he'd experienced at their handshake hadn't prepared him for this wicked snap of desire. Afterward, he wasn't sure which of them was more shocked. They gaped at each other as Molly studied her nails.

"Speechless?" Jonas prodded as he awaited Serena's comeback.

He expected whatever she said to be flippant, perhaps even rude. He'd certainly earned a cutting remark or two with his forward behavior. Though in his defense she hadn't resisted him. Not in the least. He couldn't believe he'd kissed her—or that he wanted to do it again. Her lips had lost most of their red gloss but none of their appeal.

When Serena finally spoke, she floored him with honesty.

"I'm a big enough person to admit when I'm wrong. And, *man*, was I wrong." A grin accompanied the admission.

Wrong wasn't the word for it, Serena mused inwardly as her hormones continued to pop and fizz like the bubbles in champagne. She hadn't seen this reaction coming even if she *had* found the man attractive from the get-go.

That in itself was surprising. In his charcoal suit, snowy white shirt and muted print tie, he was one hundred and eighty degrees from the artsy, anti-establishment sort who usually caught her notice. She chalked up his appeal to his handsome face, even though she'd never figured herself for being so superficial. Adonis, she'd called him.

Her gaze trailed over his broad shoulders. No doubt about it, the man worked out. She pictured him shirtless and sweaty, muscles flexing and straining as he finished up a set of curls with hand weights.

Mmm. The sound vibrated in her throat. It took Molly kicking her shin under the table for Serena to realize she was openly ogling him.

"I hope you don't mind, but I think I'm going to head back to our hotel," her friend said. She rubbed her temple as she rose to her feet. "My headache has gotten worse."

"Oh." Serena did her best to hide her disappointment as she started to rise too. "Well, Jonas, it's been…"

"Interesting?" he supplied.

Serena blew out a breath. "That's an understatement."

Molly divided her gaze between the two of them. "You should stay, Serena. I mean, if you want to."

"No. I'll go back." The words sounded half-hearted.

Their drinks arrived then. The waitress set the bourbon in front of Jonas and eyed the two women. "Who gets the dirty martini?"

Molly pointed to Serena. "Sit and have your drink."

"But…" Serena glanced at Jonas. No doubt about it, she wanted to stay. Still, she asked, "Are you sure, Moll?"

"Positive."

After Molly had left, Serena and Jonas eyed one another in silence as they sipped their drinks. With her friend seated next to her Serena's hormones had been somewhat held in check. Now they threatened to stage a riot.

"So, where are you from?" Small talk seemed the safest bet.

"Vegas, born and raised. You?"

Growing up, Serena had lived all over the world, thanks to her father's naval appointments. Southern California had been the final stop, and despite her flighty nature she'd been eager to put down roots. She and Jayne had that in common, since Jayne's father was also career military.

"I call San Diego home these days."

"Nice city. Great beaches and a pretty decent night life."

"Do you get there often?"

"No. I've only been once when I was in college."

His answer disappointed her. Ridiculously, she'd hoped he was a frequent visitor. Maybe then there would be a chance they would see each other again after tonight.

"I didn't think Vegas had many natives," she said.

Jonas smiled. "There are a few of us around—and, in case you're wondering, we don't all work in the casinos."

"You never did say what you do for a living," she reminded him.

"I'm an attorney."

Attorney. She'd never been hot for an attorney before. She'd avoided them on principle, unless they were the pro-bono sort, who wore sandals and hemp clothing and worked for worthwhile causes.

"From the look on your face, I take it you're not a fan of the profession." Before she could answer, he added, "I probably shouldn't mention my political aspirations, then."

An attorney *and* a politician? How much more pro-establishment could one get? And why wasn't Serena rising to her feet and beating a hasty retreat?

Instead, she sipped her drink and said, "Tell me about these political aspirations of yours."

"I'm running for Mayor of Las Vegas."

"No kidding?" At his nod, she asked, "Why? I mean, what made you decide you wanted to do this?"

"I have something to offer." He sipped his drink. "There's more to this city than tourism and casinos. The people who live here have legitimate concerns, as does the business community."

As Jonas spoke, Serena studied him. All that passion, and it went well beyond his kissing ability. But then hadn't he already warned her that appearances could be deceiving?

"What about you? What line of work are you in?"

"I decorate cakes."

She held her breath, half expecting him to make a derogatory remark. Her current choice of profession was a keen disappointment to her parents, and they made it plain every chance they got. But Jonas smiled broadly. She liked the way his cheeks creased when he did.

"No kidding? That's a sweet job." She groaned at the bad pun, which he apparently anticipated, because he raised his shoulders in a shrug and apologized. "I couldn't resist. So, what do you like most about your profession?"

She didn't have to think about it. "The creative aspect. Customers come into the shop and say they want a cake for their boss's retirement party, or their son's christening, or whatever. They give me a list of that person's hobbies, and sometimes they suggest a theme or a color scheme. From that, I create a cake."

"Edible artwork?"

She nodded. He got it. "Exactly."

Two hours and a second dirty martini later, Serena knew she should be going. But she didn't want the evening to end. That was as perplexing as it was terrifying. Her last half-dozen relationships—if they even could be classified as such—had fizzled out fast. Usually by the end of the first date, or at least by the second, she was eager to find an escape hatch. Serena liked men, but she wasn't willing to entrust her long-term happiness to one. She had only to look at her parents to understand why. Susanne and Buck Warren had made it their life's mission these past thirty years to make one another miserable. And, since misery loved company, they'd made their only child's life hell, too.

"You're frowning," Jonas remarked.

"I'm just wondering where the time went."

"I know." His laughter was bemused. "I came in here planning to grab a quick drink before heading home. I was wound up, yet exhausted."

"Long day?"

"Endless."

"But here you are."

"Here I am." He smiled. "And I'm not tired at all."

"It's the scintillating conversation," she teased.

In addition to more substantial topics, such as his reasons for running for public office and her plans to open her own cake shop, their conversation had leaned toward the ridiculous. They'd hashed out the lyrics to *The Flintstones* theme song, agreed on which

Stooge was the funniest—Curly, by far—and debated the merits of "innie" bellybuttons versus "outies."

Yet Jonas was perfectly serious now when he said, "I can't remember the last time I had so much fun. I've enjoyed talking with you."

"I've enjoyed talking with you, too."

"This isn't like me." He fiddled with the edge of his cocktail napkin, rolling it up until it stayed curled. "I don't usually strike up a conversation with a stranger in a bar, much less kiss her." He glanced up. "It's nuts, but I feel like I know you so well, and I don't even know your last name."

"It's Warren."

"Mine's Benjamin."

"Well, Jonas Benjamin, for the record, I don't normally let strange men kiss me in a bar."

"I'm glad you made an exception."

The creases in his cheeks reappeared when he smiled, and her stomach took a funny tumble. "Same goes."

A long moment passed before he said, "Technically, we're no longer strangers. So, if I were to kiss you again…" He left the thought unfinished, but his gaze was now focused on her mouth.

Anticipation began to build. Their last kiss hadn't been nearly enough to satisfy her curiosity, or anything else.

Just as Serena started to lean forward, a hand slapped a little black folder down on the table between them. She and Jonas sat back abruptly. Their waitress had appeared from nowhere.

"I'll take your bill up whenever you're ready," the woman said.

"Gee, I think that's our cue to leave," Serena murmured, realizing for the first time that the bar was nearly empty.

"It's almost closing time. You probably should be getting back to your hotel," Jonas said. He pulled out his wallet and laid some bills on the table. Afterward, he stood and pulled out her chair—a gentlemanly gesture the likes of which she'd rarely experienced. But then the whole evening had been a trek through uncharted territory.

Once they were outside, instead of heading in the direction of McKendrick's, Jonas stopped, stuffed his hands in his pockets and rocked back on his heels. He looked nervous—hopeful when he said. "You know, I'm kind of hungry."

Her heart fluttered. "Now that you mention it, so am I."

"Maybe we could grab a bite before we call it a night? I know this great retro diner within walking distance of here that makes the best cheeseburgers around."

"I love cheeseburgers." She slipped her hand into his. This time she was ready for the sparks the contact generated and she reveled in them.

"Crazy, huh?" he said.

Serena didn't have to ask what he meant. "Outrageous—and, believe me, I know outrageous."

The pair of them were so different—he classic Brooks Brothers and she unapologetically offbeat. Yet they were in tune with one another. So much so that a couple of hours later, when they started back from the diner, their strides matched and their arms swung in unison.

They stopped in front of the Bellagio's illuminated fountains. Back where it all began, Serena mused. Somehow she knew her life was never going to be the same. As they watched the water shoot up Jonas turned. He'd kissed her several times since first leaving the Bellagio, each kiss longer and more enticing than the last. Even so they'd left her yearning for more. She couldn't get enough of him, and not just physically. This went beyond being turned on.

Instead of kissing her now, he took her in his arms and danced with her in the moonlight, ending with a dip that left her nearly parallel to the ground. His unexpected turn as Fred Astaire charmed her, and left them both laughing, but afterward, when he held her in his arms, his grasp was just this side of desperate. She understood perfectly. Over his shoulder she watched the water arc in the air, every bit as enchanting as their time together.

"Tonight has been magical," he said, as if he could read her mind.

Serena hummed in agreement. "I wish it didn't have to end."

"Does it?"

His answer surprised her. She pulled back far enough so she could see his face. "Doesn't it?"

"I don't know." The way Jonas frowned gave the impression he rarely found himself without an answer. Yet he struggled for one now. "You…us…on the surface it doesn't make any sense."

"Not much, no. But someone recently reminded me that appearances can be deceiving."

Serena laughed, but he was still frowning. "When I saw you I had the strangest feeling that I knew you—that I'd been—"

"Looking for you," she supplied as her heart bucked out a couple of extra beats. "What happens now?"

"Normally I'd say goodnight, give myself a few days to think and put things in perspective."

"I return to San Diego in less than twelve hours." She pulled out of his embrace and despite the evening's heat felt chilled immediately. "Got another idea?"

He frowned again. "Yes, but it's…" He shook his head and looked a little dazed. "It's crazy."

A grin tugged at Serena's lips. "I'm always up for crazy."

He didn't smile. He swallowed, and she watched his Adam's apple bob. "This qualifies as insane, even if in a totally weird way it makes perfect sense."

"Well, don't keep me in suspense."

He inhaled deeply. "You could stay."

Serena barely heard his words over the pounding of her heart. "Stay? In Vegas?" she said, to be sure she hadn't imagined the offer. After Jonas nodded, she asked, "For how long?"

He did smile now, and his expression was that of a gambler letting his fortune ride on the roll of the dice.

"How about forever?"

CHAPTER TWO

WHAT had she done?

Serena woke in the strange hotel room with a start. Clutching the sheet to her chest, she jack-knifed to a sitting position and turned her head. Even knowing what she would find, she felt her mouth gape open at the sight that greeted her.

Oh. My. God!

It hadn't been a dream. Jonas Benjamin was splayed out on his side of the bed beside her—shirtless and then some. Since his eyes were closed, she allowed her gaze to follow the length of his spine down his nicely muscled back. The sheet interfered with her view when it reached his hips, but what she couldn't see now she clearly remembered seeing—and touching—last night. With her memory working overtime, Serena became uncomfortably aware of her own nakedness.

It wasn't the vivid recollections of their passionate lovemaking that had her panicking. It was what had happened just prior to it. Jonas's right hand was tucked beneath the pillow, but his left one was clearly visible, and the third finger sported a cheap band identical to the one on hers.

They were married!

The magic of the previous night leaked away, leaving stark reality in its place. She, the woman who couldn't commit to anything, had stood in a tacky Vegas chapel and promised to love, honor and cherish for a lifetime a man she hadn't even known for a day.

It was only in the past year that she'd committed to a hair color, going back to her natural red after trying out shades that ran the gamut from Goth black to punk purple. Or that she'd committed to a job. She'd worked full-time decorating cakes at the upscale Bonaventure Creations in La Jolla for a solid eleven months—a record on her part, especially since she still loved it. But marriage? She couldn't do marriage—even if for a brief time last night it had seemed like a really good idea.

Serena smothered a groan with her hand. She'd done a lot of bone-headed things in her life. Leaping without looking was a specialty of hers. But this wouldn't be as easy to fix as the bad neon-green dye job she'd sported two St Patrick's Days ago. Nor would it be as easy to hide as the dragonfly tattoo that hovered low on her right hip—the result of one too many margaritas on her twenty-first birthday.

What was she going to do?

Her gaze followed the trail of their discarded clothing back to the room's door. The only thing that came through loud and clear was she needed to leave. Now. Before Jonas woke. Before he smiled and said something sweet or funny. Before he was able to change her mind. Because maybe he could…for a little while anyway.

His tie caught her notice. It hung from the corner of the headboard. Serena frowned as she studied it. They were so different. Too different. Likely upon his waking reality would smack the professional and very put-together Jonas Benjamin upside the head, as it had her, and he would be as eager as she was to extricate himself from this situation.

Pride demanded she be the one to leave first. Serena slipped from the bed and gathered up what she could find of her clothing. A few minutes later she was dressed, minus her bra and one of her earrings. She heard him stir as she bent to slip a hastily penned note of explanation into one of his size-eleven wingtips.

"Who...who's there?" he called sleepily.

He didn't even recall her name! Her heart sank even as her resolve strengthened.

"Nobody worth remembering," she whispered, and closed the door.

The lock snicked shut before Jonas made it off the bed. Cursing, he flopped back on the mattress, rubbed the sleep from his eyes and tried to get his bearings. The events of the previous evening came back to him with the force of a fast-moving freight train and made him grateful to already be prone.

Serena. His wife.

He'd only gotten a peek at her pale face before the door closed, but he knew this much for certain: she wasn't going out for coffee and bagels. She'd bolted.

He wasn't sure how he felt about that. Truth be told, he wasn't sure how he felt about *anything*. He'd married a woman he'd known for a handful of hours. Talk about acting out of character. He preferred his Is dotted, his Ts neatly crossed. Tidy and well-ordered—that was how he liked his life. Every move he'd made since graduating from law school had been planned out carefully and methodically. Or every move until he'd walked into that lounge the previous night and spied a vivacious redhead. For a handful of stolen hours she'd been his sole reality. He hadn't lost himself in a woman like that ever. As thrilling and baffling as he'd found the sensation the evening before, right now he felt confused and oddly vulnerable.

A cellphone trilled and pulled him back to the present. The ringer was low and muffled, and came from beneath his wrinkled trousers.

"Benjamin here," he said, after retrieving it.

"Where are you?" Jameson Culver demanded by way of a greeting. "We agreed to meet first thing this morning at campaign headquarters, to go over the radio spots you'll be taping tomorrow. It's after nine."

"Ah…right. Sorry. I've been…tied up." It wasn't a complete lie, he decided as he recalled one of the inventive uses Serena had found for his necktie. His campaign manager, however, was far from mollified.

"Well, get untied," Jameson boomed. "This is important, Jonas."

As if he needed reminding. "I know my

lines forward and backward. That's the benefit of speaking from the heart."

"I want to be sure you punch the right words. Now that former Mayor Cloverfield has endorsed you, Davenport is going to pull out all the stops to discredit you. You need to come across as confident and authoritative. He's going to keep hitting on your youth and relative political inexperience. He's going to make it seem as if you're trying to cash in on your family's name recognition with voters in this region."

"This election is about me." Jonas had gone out of his way to keep his father out of his campaign. All of his life he'd lived in his father's shadow. He wanted to win on his own merit.

"Maybe you should ask Corbin to do a commercial spot. His public endorsement could sway some of the fence-sitters," Jameson said.

"No. Absolutely not."

"You've pulled ahead a little in the polls after last week's town hall debate, but it's still anyone's race."

"I know that." The words came out sharp.

Jameson wasn't deterred. "There's a strategy for winning elections. Hand-shaking

and baby-kissing only get you so far. Your
father is political gold, Jonas."

"My answer remains no."

His campaign manager sighed dramati-
cally. "Fine, but keep this in mind. Voters say
they want change, but when it comes right
down to it they often go with what they know.
Davenport's work on the council makes him
less of a mystery. You're untried, Jonas,
which means they want to know anything
and everything there is to know about you."

A lead weight settled in the pit of Jonas's
stomach as he spied the white envelope sticking
out of one his shoes. "About that…" he began.

"Is there a problem?"

"I'm not sure."

After ending the call, Jonas dressed. His
clothes were a little the worse for wear,
though not in as sorry a state as the lacey
lavender bra he discovered under his shirt. It
hooked in the front. He remembered helping
Serena out of it and helping himself to…

He closed his eyes, groaned, and lowered
himself to the side of the mattress. Unfortunately he misjudged his proximity and found
himself on the floor instead. Appropriate,
he decided. He'd been off-balance since
meeting the woman.

"Might as well get this over with," he muttered. Wedging the tip of his index finger beneath the flap, he unsealed the envelope and sealed his fate.

Dear Jonas,
I don't know where to begin.

"Yeah, join the club." He snorted, bemused to find them once again in perfect agreement.

Sorry doesn't seem the right word, but it's the only one I can come up with. I had a lovely time last night. An amazing time, in fact. But I got carried away. I think we both did. Marriage!

Of course, this is Vegas. I'm sure we're not the only two people to ever find themselves caught up in the moment. Since you're a lawyer, I assume you will know what to do to remedy the matter. I will pay half of any legal fees, etc.

I am returning to San Diego today as planned. Forgive me for not waking you up to say goodbye. I thought it would be easier and less embarrassing for both of us if I just left.

Thanks seems as awkward a word

as sorry, but it fits here. You are a very special man and I wish you nothing but the best.
—*Serena*

She'd listed her contact information at the bottom of the page, along with a postscript:

I'm returning the ring. I know it wasn't expensive, but perhaps you can get your money back.

He fished the band out of the envelope. It was a cheap piece of metal that had probably already caused her flesh to turn green. He slipped off the one on his finger and, on an oath, flung them both into the wastebasket on the opposite side of the room.

Still sitting on the floor, he rested an elbow on one raised knee and stared at the note. Serena's penmanship was as eclectic as the woman: a collection of capital and lowercase block letters with some cursive ones tossed in. The dots for the "i"s were misaligned or missing. The "t"s were half crossed. He should have been pleased that she didn't want to stay married to him, grateful that she was making this so easy for him. No tears. No demands, financial or otherwise, and God knew he'd left himself wide open to those. No repercussions of any sort.

Jonas let his head fall back on the mattress and closed his eyes as he waited for the relief to come. Any moment a huge wave of it would wash over him and cleanse the last reminders of Serena Warren from his memory.

More than a dozen hours later, when he collapsed on the bed in his downtown condo, he still wasn't completely sure relief was among his tangled-up emotions.

CHAPTER THREE

SERENA woke late on Monday morning. According to her sorry excuse for an alarm clock she was already forty minutes behind schedule. Even so, she sat on the side of the bed and contemplated the state of her life. The day before she'd awoken in a deluxe Vegas honeymoon suite next to a virtual stranger who was also her husband. This morning she was alone on the lumpy bed of her San Diego studio, but the man in question was very much on her mind.

How was Jonas?

The question sneaked past her defenses and brought along a couple of friends. Was Jonas angry with her? Or was he relieved that she'd offered him an uncomplicated way out?

Serena was relieved, or so she told herself. Maybe she was a little disappointed that she hadn't heard from him, but only because she wanted to know his plans. Still, it made sense that he hadn't called yet. It had been barely twenty-four hours, and even in Vegas she doubted the courthouses were open on Sundays. Surely first thing today Jonas would go and file whatever paperwork needed to be filed to get the ball rolling to dissolve their marriage.

Maybe she should call him and make sure they were of the same mind. The office where he practiced law would be easy enough to locate through directory assistance, or she could always ask for the number for his campaign headquarters.

As she picked up the phone, Serena imagined a well-mannered receptionist asking, *And who may I say is calling, please?* She set the receiver back in its cradle with a click. She didn't have the time or, she admitted, the courage to talk to him right now. What she did have was someplace to be. And she needed to get there before her boss, the highly regarded but annoyingly high-strung Heidi Bonaventure, blew a gasket.

Twenty minutes later, with a silver travel mug of high-octane java in hand, Serena flung open her apartment door, intending to make a mad dash for the stairs. She didn't make it past the welcome mat. Indeed, she stopped so abruptly that despite the mug's protective lid some of her coffee spewed through the small opening. It hit Jonas Benjamin in the center of his sedately striped tie. Counting the silk number she'd mutilated in her haste to undress him two nights ago, this made two she'd ruined.

She grimaced. "What are you doing here?"

"Hoping to have the conversation we should have had yesterday morning," he replied. He didn't look happy.

They eyed one another from opposite sides of the welcome mat. Neither one of them moved.

Serena cleared her throat and broke the silence. "You came all the way to San Diego to talk about our...our..."

"Marriage," he supplied.

Annulment was the word she'd been thinking.

"About yesterday—sorry for taking off like that, but I...I..." In lieu of an excuse Serena motioned with her hand.

Unfortunately it was the one holding the travel mug. More java splattered out. Jonas jumped back in the nick of time, and the welcome mat was the only casualty. She pushed at one of the brown marks with the toe of her faux snakeskin flat. It was easier to concentrate on the stain than the man whose head had rested on the pillow next to hers twenty-four hours earlier.

"Can I come in?" Jonas asked.

"I'm just on my way out. To work."

"Can you be late?"

"Actually, I already am."

"Can you be later?" Jonas tucked his hands into his trouser pockets. The pose took away some of the formalness the pricy suit added to his persona. "This really can't wait, Serena."

"I know." She stepped back to allow him inside and motioned toward the couch. This time she remembered to use the hand that wasn't holding her coffee. "Make yourself at home. It will just take me a moment to call my boss."

While he took a seat on the couch, Serena stationed herself in the kitchen and pulled out her cellphone. Her apartment measured just over four hundred square feet. It was basically one room, with a bathroom tucked between the kitchen and bedroom areas. This created some separation, as well as a degree of privacy, for her boudoir from the door. But from Jonas's vantage point he could see everything—including the pile of dirty clothes that was heaped next to the still-down bed with its rumpled sheets and her discarded cotton nightie.

She hadn't worn a nightie, cotton or otherwise, in Vegas. Even if she'd had one with her in the honeymoon suite, what would have been the point? None of their clothes had remained on for long. They'd been too hungry, too eager, too desperate to touch flesh.

"Oh, God," she moaned.

"No. It's Heidi Bonaventure." A woman's crisp voice shot through the phone line like a bullet.

"Mrs. Bonaventure, hi. It's Serena."

"I hope you're not calling to say you're ill."

Her boss was a whiz when it came to crafting lifelike fruit from marzipan, and her piping work was unrivaled, but no one would accuse Heidi Bonaventure of being warm and fuzzy.

"No. I'll be there. Just not for another hour." Serena glanced over at Jonas, who sat on the edge of her red leather sofa. One wingtip tapped impatiently on the floor, and he hadn't so much as loosened his stained tie. "Or so."

Heidi's voice no longer sounded like a bullet. It boomed with the force of a bomb as she reminded Serena, "You have an appointment with a client at eleven o'clock. Katherine Bloomwell requested you specifically to create her daughter's sweet-sixteen cake."

"I won't miss the appointment," Serena promised. "But something important has come up."

"What could be more important than your job?"

She glanced over at Jonas again. This time their gazes met and, just as she had in Las Vegas, she felt that wild jolt.

Heidi's voice snapped her back to the matter at hand. "Given your serious lack of experience and formal training, I took a huge chance when I hired you."

Actually, she'd hired Serena as a glorified gopher slash receptionist. She'd only given Serena her current responsibilities out of necessity nine months ago, when her assistant had quit without notice, leaving Heidi in the lurch. Serena had shown promise and an eagerness to learn, staying late without pay if it meant acquiring new skills. Indeed, she was still paid the same lowly amount she'd made coming in. She wisely chose not to point any of this out as her boss's tirade continued.

"Since then I've offered you the sort of opportunities that many a culinary arts student would kill for. Don't make me regret it."

"I won't."

"See that you don't."

"I'll be there as soon as I can, and I promise I'll arrive before the client does."

Heidi snorted. "See that you do. In the meantime, I suggest you rethink your priorities."

"Everything okay?" Jonas called from the couch as Serena dropped her cellphone on the counter.

"Fine. Just my boss." She rolled her eyes. "She's better at making me squirm than my mother is. And, believe me, that's saying a lot."

His smile was awkward. Because he'd gotten her into hot water at work? Or because she'd mentioned the woman who was, for the time being at least, his mother-in-law? Serena wasn't sure which. She only knew she felt awkward now, too.

"So…" She took a seat on the thick-armed chair that was perpendicular to the couch, discreetly brushing aside a stray popcorn kernel.

"So…" he repeated, and folded his hands over one knee.

Two nights ago the conversation had flowed endlessly, seamlessly. Now neither of them could string together a complete sentence. Clearing her throat, Serena attempted it again. "How long…um…will it take to, you know, undo what we did?"

Though the question was far from eloquent, she figured her meaning was clear. Jonas frowned, though, as he repeated, "Undo what we did?"

"Yeah. Undo the…um…the 'I do' part." She laughed nervously.

He studied her a moment, before rising to his feet. Then he paced to the sliding doors that led to the studio's small balcony. When he turned to face her he was no longer frowning, but his expression was far from pleased.

"I'm afraid there's a bit of a situation—a hitch."

"To our getting unhitched? Sorry." She scrunched up her face. Nerves had her saying stupid things. "Go on."

"I'm not sure how to put this."

"Well, whatever it is, say it fast—like you're pulling off a bandage," she suggested. Between his hesitation and turned-down lips her stomach was starting to churn like one of the commercial-grade mixers at the bakery.

"Okay, here it is. I want to stay married to you."

She couldn't have heard him right, Serena decided, which was why it took her a moment to realize that her mouth was gaping open.

Jonas tried to determine Serena's reaction to his words. Beyond flummoxed, he couldn't be sure. He took the fact that she wasn't smiling, however, to mean she wasn't thrilled with the idea. After the way she'd ditched him in Vegas the previous morning, he hadn't exactly expected her to be. He ignored the vague sense of disappointment he felt, and assumed what one of his law school professors had called the litigator pose. Clasping his hands behind his back, he paced in front of the balcony doors.

"We don't know one another well, but as you may recall from our conversations the other evening I'm currently running for election in Las Vegas."

"Mayor," she said.

He nodded. Good. She remembered that much.

"A lot of people, especially in the business community, believe your opponent lacks the imagination and vision to expand on the revitalization efforts that are currently underway."

Jonas blinked. "I…yes."

Her green gaze locked on him. "Surprised I was paying attention?"

He shrugged. "Politics can be dry—and, well, other parts of our evening were far more memorable than discussions of my candidacy."

One side of her mouth quirked up. "Now, there's an understatement."

Serena was seated demurely enough, her legs crossed at the ankles. But for a moment a vision of her wearing nothing but his crumpled tie, with those long legs clamped around his waist, blasted free from his memory.

"Yeah."

He took a step toward her, then remembered why he was there. He needed her to do him a favor. His political life could very well depend on it.

"Anyway, marriages are a matter of public record. As such, ours is guaranteed to become fodder for my opponent in pretty short order. This isn't your problem, but once it's out things could get ugly for my campaign."

"How so?"

"Well, for starters, no one has ever met you. Nor have we ever been seen together. Add in the fact that my bachelor status has been duly noted in all of the previous profiles the media have done on me and..."

"It gets ugly," she finished.

The afternoon before, his campaign manager's face had turned a worrying shade of purple when Jonas had told him about Serena and their impromptu nuptials. The two of them had come up with an idea to salvage his political ambitions. It had seemed plausible then—reasonable, even. Right now, as he stared at Serena's full lips, it not only seemed absurd but self-serving.

He blurted it out anyway. "I need for us to remain married."

"For political purposes?"

"Yes."

Serena was wearing a bright yellow silk tunic with elaborate beading and embroidery around the neckline. The rich flecks of green, purple and red suited her. She ran one hand over it absently now, apparently weighing his words.

"But we would go our separate ways eventually, right? We wouldn't stay married…till death do us part."

They'd already made that promise. He'd been sincere at the time. He wasn't the sort to make a promise knowing he would break it. In the cold light of day, however, it seemed ridiculous to think either one of them could keep it. Sincerity aside, they barely knew one another.

"No. Not that long," he assured her.

"How long?" She nibbled that plump bottom lip.

He remembered her doing the same just the other night.

"Jonas?" Her voice interrupted the memory. She didn't look pleased with the prospect of remaining his wife, even if their stint of matrimony came with an early get-out clause.

"That depends."

A pair of green eyes narrowed. "On?"

"The outcome of the general election. In the past the Mayor's race has been decided in June, but this year the clerk's office opted to go with an election cycle similar to a lot of other municipalities."

"November," she said. "So, if I agree, we would remain married until November."

He cleared his throat. "Again, that depends. If I lose—" he shrugged "—that can be the end of it. We go our separate ways. An annulment, especially since we both want it and I'm already a resident of Las Vegas, can be handled quietly. By the time it's public record I'll be old news."

"And if you win?" Her gaze remained direct.

"We would have to stay married a little longer. It would look pretty suspect if my bride ditched me the day after I was sworn into office." He offered a charming smile to cover his desperation and the uncomfortable realization that she'd already ditched him once.

"How long, Jonas?"

"For… For…"

Forever. That was how long he'd asked her to stay the other night. He shoved the thought away now, no longer sure that was what he wanted, even if it were possible, and given the way she'd dashed from their hotel room it didn't look likely.

After clearing his throat, he said, "I don't have a timeframe etched in stone. A few months or so."

Actually, Jameson had insisted on at least a year. That length of time, he'd said, would help silence the skeptics and create sympathy for Jonas when the marriage dissolved, upping his chances for a successful first term and re-election if he chose to run again. Since Serena appeared to be on the fence, Jonas decided a little vagueness was in order. The length of time was negotiable.

"What would I have to do? A few public appearances? Kiss a baby or two?"

There was more to it than that—press interviews and the like—but he nodded. "Sure."

"I guess I could fly up on weekends, and maybe here and there during the week if you had a special engagement that you need me to attend in the evening." She grimaced, glanced away. "I'd...um...need some help covering travel expenses, though. My budget is pretty tight right now, and I'm not due a raise for a while."

Jonas scratched his cheek. "Here's the thing. To make it believable, you couldn't stay in San Diego and commute up now and then. You'd have to live in Las Vegas. With me." He swallowed. Only after saying it aloud did he consider all of the ramifications and disturbing possibilities of setting up a household with her.

Serena blinked a few times in rapid succession. "Let me get this straight. Not only are you asking me to put off our annulment, you want me to move to Las Vegas and live with you as your wife for the foreseeable future?"

"Yes." At her raised eyebrows, he added, "It's a lot to ask, I know."

"A lot? Gee, you're just full of understatements today. What about my apartment, Jonas?" She motioned wide with her arms. "What about my job?"

"I'll continue to pay the lease, or if you'd

prefer you can sublet it." The job was more difficult, but he'd anticipated it being a stumbling block so had an answer ready. "As for the job, I think you should quit."

He hadn't known Serena long, but in their short time together he'd seen her experience dozens of emotions. Rage was new. And, damn, it looked good on her.

"So you think I should quit?" she began slowly, softly. Both the pace and volume of her words picked up considerably when she continued. "Because *you* find *yourself* in a bind, and because *your* dream job is on the line, *you* think I should be more than happy to throw in the towel on the only job I've ever found that I can see myself doing five years, hell, twenty years from now?"

"Serena—"

She talked over him. "I don't suppose any of that matters to you. Decorating cakes isn't rocket science. Certainly it's not as important as running for public office," she drawled.

"Serena—"

"Or maybe you share my parents' attitude that this is just a fad and will wind up as one more gig on my long and eclectic résumé?" She exhaled sharply and her eyes turned bright. "When I told them I wanted to open my own cake shop someday they laughed."

"I'm not laughing." Jonas crossed to her, and though he knew it wasn't wise he touched her, cupping her elbows and drawing her closer. "You told me your dream the other night. I didn't laugh then. I'm not laughing now. It's important to you. That's obvious." She was wearing the same perfume she'd had on when they met. No florals for her. It was citrusy, bold. It made it hard to think. Jonas forced himself to stay focused. "I'm not asking you to give up your dream."

"Good, because I won't." Her chin notched up. "Even in the short time I've been at Bonaventure I've made a name for myself. Today I'm meeting with a client who specifically requested me, and that's not the first time it's happened—despite my lack of professional training. If I quit now, it would be like starting from scratch."

"Your current position and the business you'd like to one day own are not mutually exclusive, Serena."

"One leads to the other."

"Not with the right financing and contacts."

That got her attention. Wary green eyes studied him. "What do you mean?"

"What if I could guarantee access to both at the end of our…arrangement?" The word left a sour taste in his mouth, but he plodded ahead. "What if, between now and then, you were able to—I don't know—maybe take some classes and get some of the training you say you're lacking? After we…um… wrap things up, I could set you up with a list of potential clients and the capital to start your own shop."

"That sounds like…" He waited for the word *heaven*, or something along that line. Serena's take on the matter was, "Prostitution!"

She shook free of his grasp and marched half a dozen steps away. Rage was back, and though it looked good on her he didn't want to see it now.

"I realize the oldest profession is legal in some parts of your state, but if I wanted to sell myself in order to open my own cake shop I could do that here, Jonas. No pimp necessary."

She wasn't the only one angry now. He wrenched at his tie, since it seemed to be constricting his windpipe. "That's not the kind of arrangement I'm suggesting!"

She crossed her arms and blinked slowly in challenge. "No?"

"No! What I'm suggesting, what I'm *offering*, is a business opportunity. Nothing more. Nothing less."

The shouted words echoed in the tiny apartment. If Jameson, the self-proclaimed king of spin, were on hand to witness the exchange, he would be sorely disappointed in his protégé. Jonas had botched this, and badly. He fully expected Serena to tell him to go to hell and then show him the door.

"Let's be clear on one thing. I don't want your money. I'm not looking for a shortcut to a big payday—especially one that involves selling my soul or anything else."

"I know." He shoved a hand through his hair and expelled a breath. "I apologize if what I'm offering sounded like payment for services rendered. That wasn't my intention. It's just that I felt that since I was getting something of obvious value out of the proposed arrangement, you should, too. And I know how much you enjoy having free creative reign when it comes to decorating cakes."

"You know?"

"You aren't the only one who was listening the other night."

That took the wind out of her sails. "How is it possible that you get it?" she asked softly.

"Excuse me?"

She shook her head. "Nothing. I...it's madness."

"Would offering you a low-interest loan make the offer more palatable?"

"Jonas, I...I don't know. God! I can barely think." She rested her fingertips against her temples. "And here I thought my life had been turned upside down in Vegas."

"It's chaotic right now," he agreed. "But I think we can make it work. In the end, this doesn't need to be a huge mistake."

"A huge mistake?" She pressed the heels of her hands to her eyes. "I need time to be sure I'm not making another one if I agree."

"Of course." The vise around his heart eased its grip.

"How long are you in town?" The question was slightly muffled by her pose.

"I just flew down for the morning. I have meetings this afternoon, some radio spots to tape. If you...if you decide to come back to Las Vegas I'll return for you Friday."

Her hands dropped away at that. The green eyes regarding him were wide and incredulous.

"*This* Friday?"

"I wish I could give you more time, Serena. But a civic group called Las Vegas Citizens for Change is putting on a dinner Saturday evening, and my opponent and I have both been invited to attend. Jameson thinks—"

"Jameson?"

"Culver. He's my campaign manager. He thinks you and I should go to the dinner together and make the big announcement of our marriage there. Take the offensive, so to speak, before anyone else gets wind of it, twists it around and makes more of it than there is." He felt his face heat. "You know what I mean."

"Yeah." Her gaze shifted to the wall. "I know what you mean."

"I'm sorry, Serena. I wish…" Jonas left the thought unfinished. No sense getting into what he wished, since he wasn't sure he knew.

"It's not your fault," she said.

"Yours either." Most definitely none of this fell on her shoulders. Even so, she tried to take the blame.

"I don't know about that. I'm pretty well known for acting on a whim and dragging others with me." Serena motioned toward his conservatively cut suit. "Despite that first… um…*crazy* kiss in the Bellagio, you still don't strike me as the sort of man who does anything impulsive."

"Not usually, no. But I'm an adult, Serena. You didn't drag me anywhere I didn't want to go. At the time."

She nodded. "At the time."

CHAPTER FOUR

SERENA collapsed onto the sofa with a groan after Jonas had left. What should she do? If she accepted his proposal—his *second* proposal—she had only a matter of days to sublet her apartment, pack up her belongings, quit her job at Bonaventure Creations, and inform her friends and family that not only was she married, she was moving to Vegas.

She nibbled a fingernail—a habit she'd broken two decades earlier.

Should she tell them *everything*? Including that she and Jonas were only staying married to keep Jonas's political future alive? Gee, that would go over well with her parents. Serena could already hear her father's booming baritone.

Do you ever use your head? Do you ever think before you act?

No doubt her mother would chain-smoke

a pack of cigarettes as she demanded of no one in particular, *Where did we go wrong?*

Serena was used to their reactions. She was pretty sure she'd been a huge disappointment to her folks from the moment she'd slipped from the birth canal and the doctor had offered his congratulations on a healthy baby girl. Her father had wanted a boy. Her mother? She'd just wanted peace, and there would be none in the Warren household until Buck got his way. Unfortunately health complications had prevented Susanne from having a second child, and so the cold war had begun. It had been waging ever since, with Serena lost in the permafrost.

Well, no matter. She could deal with her parents' disappointment and censure. Nothing new there. But what were her friends going to think?

She nibbled a second fingernail.

She wasn't as concerned that they would be disappointed in her judgment. Their love, unlike her parents', was unconditional. But they might be angry or hurt that she'd failed to tell them about her hasty nuptials to begin with.

Resting her head on the back of the sofa, Serena studied a quarter-sized indentation on the ceiling. A shooting champagne cork the previous New Year's Eve was responsible. Alex, who'd opened the bottle, had apologized profusely and insisted on paying to fix the damage. Serena had waved off the offer. It gave the place character, to her way of thinking. But it would have to be patched before she moved out if she hoped to get her security deposit back.

The four women had drunk a toast to the mark then, and another celebrating their friendship. A couple of hours later, minus Jayne, who'd gone off to dinner with her fiancé, they'd rung in the New Year with another bottle of equally poor-quality sparkling wine. The good, the bad and the ugly. Serena had shared it all with her friends. So why hadn't she told them about Jonas when she'd returned to the hotel?

It wasn't like her to keep secrets—especially one this big, that was just begging to be picked apart and analyzed as only good friends could do. She'd told herself at the time it was because Alex's decision to stay in Vegas had been enough for them to deal with. But that was an excuse. Curiously, even Molly hadn't said a word about Serena's all-nighter.

She glanced at the clock. She needed to get to work, but tonight she would gather the troops—two physically, one by phone—beg their forgiveness if necessary, and solicit their advice.

"I still can't believe you got married." Molly shook her head before taking another sip of iced tea. "I know we were in Vegas and all, and that's the place where people do things that are…well, out of character." Her cheeks turned rosy as she said it. "But *married*?"

Serena lifted her shoulders and sent her a weak smile. "You know me."

"No, hon. *This* is wild even for you," Jayne put in. She snagged a tortilla chip from the bowl in the center of the coffee table and dipped it in salsa. Though she tried to hide it, sadness leaked into her expression when she added, "He must be something else to have turned your head so quickly and so completely."

"You met him, Molly. What's he like?" Alex asked via speakerphone.

"I wasn't with them for long, since I had a headache and it was quite obvious I was a fifth wheel." Her smile was wry. "But he seemed nice."

"He *is* nice," Serena said.

Which was why she was so torn. If Jonas were a jerk it would have been so easy to tell him no straight out when he'd showed up that morning. She wouldn't have had to involve her friends, desperate for their insight. Instead, as night fell on San Diego, she remained confused.

An hour had passed since she'd made her big announcement. At first the news had been met with utter silence. But once their initial shock had worn off the other women had pelted Serena with questions—Alex burning up the phoneline with her queries. Now they were down to the nitty-gritty of figuring out what Serena should do.

Jayne, who worked as a debt manager, was ever practical, and offered to make a list of pros and cons.

"I don't know," Serena hedged. "I'm not much of a list maker."

"In this case you need to be," Alex admonished over the phone. "You need to be sure you're making the right choice."

"She's right," Molly said. "Let's put it all down on paper and see what we've got." She rose and crossed to the overflowing desk that was tucked in the corner. After rooting around in the clutter, she came back with a notebook and pen. "Pros," she wrote, and glanced expectantly at Serena.

Serena coiled a lock of auburn hair around one finger, picturing Jonas. "Well, as I said, he's nice. He's smart, too, and surprisingly funny." Though his demeanor during their encounter earlier that day had been nothing short of grim. But in Vegas. Ah, Vegas… A sigh escaped her lips as she recalled their evening together. In a voice barely above a whisper, she said, "You wouldn't believe how well that man can kiss."

It was the wrong thing to remember, much less to say. She glanced over at Molly and Jayne. Their expressions were rife with concern. She didn't need to see Alex to know hers was the same.

"Um, Serena, we were looking for pros as to why you should agree to move to Vegas and *pretend* to be happily married to Jonas until the election," Molly said.

Jayne was more direct. "Do you think you might want to remain married to him for real?"

"No! God, no!" Serena straightened in her seat. It took an effort, but she pulled herself back from the edge of the hormonal abyss she'd all but drowned in upon meeting Jonas. "Okay, I'll admit it. I'm attracted to him. How could I not be? You saw him, Moll. Tell Jayne and Alex. The guy is way hot."

"Way hot," Molly repeated dutifully. Then, "You've met hot guys before. Remember Giovanni from last summer? Body of a god and an Italian accent that qualified as foreplay? You didn't marry *him*." Her brow puckered. "You didn't even go on a second date with him."

Serena ignored Molly's comment and tapped a finger thoughtfully to her chin.

"Okay, pros for helping Jonas out by putting off our annulment and relocating to Vegas *temporarily*," she stressed for her friends' benefit. "Alex is there. We can hang out."

"I love that idea!" Her friend's voice rang out. "Although I'm pretty swamped with work right now, and it sounds like you're going to have some obligations, too. Still, it will be good to have at least one of you here."

Serena grinned. "Write that down."

"Got it. What else?" Molly asked.

"He's offering me a chance to jumpstart my cake-decorating career."

Molly dutifully penned that one in the "pros" column as well.

"And there's the obvious one that I owe him."

Molly's hand stilled.

Jayne squinted at her and asked, "How do you figure that?"

"Hello? The man woke up in a honeymoon suite with a wedding band on his left hand," Serena replied dryly as she waggled her bare ring finger. "Not exactly rocket science."

Alex's voice cut through the silence. "You woke up in the same suite, in the same condition. Unless you're going to tell me you held a gun to his head and marched him to the nearest chapel, he put that ring on your finger of his own free will."

Molly, a kindergarten teacher, was more diplomatic in her analysis. "Serena, it's fine to take responsibility for your own actions, but there's no reason to blame yourself for his. Alex is right. Jonas is a big boy. From what you said, neither of you was inebriated when you decided to head to that chapel."

"We hadn't had a drink in hours," she agreed, although somehow the word intoxicated still applied.

"And don't forget," Molly continued, "I met Jonas. I saw the way he looked at you. I saw the way you looked at him, and the way the two of you were together. There was definite chemistry there, and that was before he kissed you."

"Definite chemistry," Serena agreed, feeling uncomfortably warm recalling the extent of it.

"But chemistry doesn't make a marriage. It just makes for a really great night."

"Isn't that the truth?" Molly murmured. Were her cheeks pink again?

"Marriage requires honesty and above all trust," Jayne put in quietly.

Serena looked at her friend's sad expression and wanted to smack herself upside the head. "God, Jayne. I'm sorry. Marriage is probably the very last thing you feel like discussing right now."

Jayne waved a hand. "It's fine. I'm fine."

Serena didn't buy that for a minute. Jayne was a long way from fine, thanks to Rich. And now Serena's penchant for getting into tight spots was only adding to her friend's misery.

"We went to Vegas to help you forget your troubles, and you wind up having to help me untangle a mess. Per usual," she snorted.

"It's all right," Jayne insisted.

"No, it's not. God, you must think me the worst sort of friend there is. And I am. The worst. The absolute worst. You need me, and instead of offering you comfort and support I've sucked you into the vortex of my own domestic drama."

Jayne pinned her with a glare. "Shut up, already. I'm not fragile. As for friendship— you should know by now it isn't a one-way street. Yes, I have needed you, and you've been there. Who talked me into going to Vegas? Who bought me my first drink when we got there? Now *you* need *me*, and I'm here."

"Thanks, Jayne."

"Don't mention it." Serena thought that was the end of it until Jayne mumbled, "The fact that your crisis followed so closely on the heels of my own is unexpected, but…"

While Alex's muffled laugh leaked over the phoneline, Molly asked, "So, any more pros?"

Two hours later she'd said goodbye to her friends. Serena was left with a sink full of dishes, a mountain of uncertainty, and a list of the reasons why she should or should not demand an immediate annulment from Jonas.

The list took up two notebook pages, much of it referring to her professional future. It seemed incredibly thorough. Only Serena knew it was woefully incomplete. She'd left a lot of things off, keeping them to herself because she couldn't bear to see them in ink.

Still, if she went with what Molly had jotted down in her tidy cursive Serena had her answer. Now she just needed to call Jonas and tell him.

* * *

Jonas's unplanned trip to San Diego had forced him to reschedule a couple of meetings with clients, and another with his campaign staff to go over canvassing strategies. Neither his clients nor Jameson Culver were particularly pleased with him, though Jameson at least was privy to the actual reason.

Though his father was still in Washington, his mother was at the family estate in suburban Las Vegas for the summer, and they'd made plans for lunch. He'd forgotten all about it until his plane had touched down in San Diego. He'd called to cancel, manufacturing an excuse about a question-and-answer interview with a local group running long. Lying to his mom didn't sit well. It occurred to him then that if Serena accepted his proposal he would be lying to voters and to all of the people who'd already thrown their support behind his candidacy.

Flipping his TV to the Sports channel, he wondered why it didn't seem that way.

Though the hour was late, Jonas had been home only forty minutes. He was still wearing a white dress shirt, albeit untucked, and gabardine trousers. He'd toed off his wingtips and shed the tailored jacket upon walking through the door of his condo. His stained tie was somewhere on the floor between the kitchen and living room. He'd find it later, or his housekeeper would. Either way, it was the least of his worries now.

The telephone rang as he nursed a beer and caught the final inning of a major league baseball game. His exhaustion was such that he couldn't even muster outrage at the umpire's bum call at home plate. Every last cobweb was shaken from his head, however, when he heard Serena's voice.

"I hope I'm not disturbing you," she began.

She was. Disturbing him in ways he didn't care to analyze, which made it easier to assure her that she wasn't. "I'm just watching the ballgame."

He pictured her in her tiny box of an apartment. Was she watching television, too? If so, was she doing it from the bed that pulled down from the wall? And what was she wearing? Thankfully her reply pulled his carnal thoughts up short.

"Oh. I'm not a fan of the actual game, but I once made a cake for a boy's tenth birthday that was shaped like a catcher's mitt, with a ball tucked in the pocket."

"Yeah? Lucky kid. I had a chocolate layer cake for my tenth birthday that had a clown face on one side. I hate clowns. They scared the hell out of me when I was a kid. I'm still not too crazy about them."

"I've never been a clown person either," she sympathized.

Silence stretched after that. Baseball, birthday cakes and their mutual dislike of clowns weren't what she'd called to talk about and they both knew it.

Finally she said, "I've done a lot of thinking about…everything."

"Oh?" He swore he could hear the blood whoosh and thump in his temples as he waited for her to continue.

"I also talked to my friends."

"The ones you came to Vegas with?"

"Yes. They're like the sisters I never had. I trust their judgment."

"Don't you trust your own?" he asked.

"Let's just say that my friends tend to be a little more grounded than I am."

"Oh." Unable to decide if that was a good thing or a bad thing where he was concerned, Jonas took another pull of his beer. He heard her clear her throat.

"There are several sound reasons why delaying our annulment and pretending to be happy newlyweds would be a bad idea." *Uh-*

oh. As he began to mentally prepare his rebuttal, Serena went on. "First of all, it's a complete fabrication."

"Is it?" Jonas wondered if he'd asked the question of Serena or himself.

"Come on, Jonas. We hardly know one another. We met two nights ago in a lounge. Are you...are you telling me it was love it first sight?"

It was *something* at first sight, but away from her and removed from the desperation of that night he was once again too practical to believe love could strike like a lightning bolt. It was built slowly and surely, layer upon layer. When one had enough layers, something solid upon which to stand, one proposed marriage. Jonas's last serious relationship had ended a month prior to his announcement that he would run for Mayor. And that had been after five years of careful layering. Despite the length of time, he hadn't felt secure enough about a future with Janet Kinkaid to propose when she'd issued an ultimatum.

He frowned. Just what had made him ask Serena to become his wife? He had no answer for either of them. It dawned on him that she was waiting.

"We hardly know one another. That's true.

But what I do know about you, Serena, I like. A lot."

"I'm sure that would change once we got to know one another," she informed him dryly.

Cynical. Hmm. He hadn't noticed that about her the other evening.

"Perhaps," he agreed. "But then we're not planning on the long-term here."

"No. Back to my point." He thought he heard papers shuffle in the background. "There are a lot of sound reasons for me to stay put in San Diego and insist on a quick annulment. Most of my friends are here, and my folks would go ballistic if they got wind of this. I have a good job. I'm learning a lot and finally getting some clients of my own. I like my apartment, and I have another nine months left on the current lease."

Even as she hammered out the reasons to decline he sensed a *but* was coming. Jonas held his breath and waited for it.

"But—" He exhaled. Thank God—there it was. "Your proposal…um…proposition is not without merit." Again he heard papers shuffle. "First of all, I wouldn't be alone in Vegas. My friend Alex just took a job there. And then there's the not-so-little matter that I feel really bad about what happened. My friends don't exactly agree, but I figure I owe it to you to help make things right. Also—"

"Whoa, whoa. Back up there, Red." Jonas set his beer on the coffee table and stood so he could pace. "You *owe* it to me?"

"Did you just call me Red?"

"I did." He stopped walking. "Problem?"

"No. I just never had a nickname. That one's not terribly original, given my hair color, but…"

He pictured a pair of sexy shoulders rising in a shrug, and enjoyed his first genuine smile in nearly thirty-six hours. Her comment about owing him, however, chased it away. She'd said something similar earlier that day, about how their situation was more her fault than his. He wanted to end that notion once and for all.

"Look, Serena, whatever you decide, don't do it out of some misplaced sense of guilt. You don't owe me anything. Your friends are completely right on that score."

"They're going to like you." She laughed before sobering. "I mean, not that we're going to be hanging out together or anything."

"Does that mean…?" He left it at that, afraid to hope.

"Yes. I'll come back to Vegas and do what needs to be done."

"I don't think it will be as grim as all that," he replied dryly.

"Sorry. You know what I mean."

"Yeah." He returned to the couch. "Thank you."

"You're welcome. And thank you. The contacts you've promised and the loan you've agreed to give me...the amount is very generous—especially since I doubt I could convince the bank to stake me anytime soon. I'll pay back every dime of it. I swear."

The loan. The business contacts. That was why she was agreeing. Jonas swallowed the disappointment that tried to creep into his tone when he replied, "No problem. I can't wait to sample some of your best work."

"Um, Jonas?"

"Yes?"

"I do have a few stipulations regarding our arrangement." Those papers shuffled ominously.

"Go on."

"First, I think we should have this all written down and spelled out clearly."

"Verbal contracts can hold up in a court of law, but I agree."

"I'm not planning to sue you or anything," she assured him. "It's just that Jayne… Rather, I think—"

"It makes sense, Serena. And since contracts are what I specialize in as a lawyer I'm a huge fan of them. They take the guesswork out of things. I'll take care of it."

"Okay."

"What else?" he asked.

"No matter what the reason—in fact, no reason is necessary—either one of us can opt out of our agreement at any time."

That didn't sit well with him, but he understood Serena's motive. She needed to feel she had choices, some control over her destiny, especially if after she arrived in Vegas she found herself in an untenable situation.

"An easy get-out clause. Got it."

"It goes without saying that should I bow out before the election I would not expect you to follow through with the loan."

He should have been happy that she was so focused on the business aspect of their relationship. Instead it was starting to annoy him.

"I'll make a note of that in the contract," he said curtly. "What else?"

"Well, it concerns our…um…personal interactions. Those…um…away from the public eye."

Jonas reached for his beer. Something told him he was going to need it. "Yes?"

"Our marriage will be in name only. No sex."

No sex?

As in none of the spectacular sex they'd enjoyed on their wedding night?

The lawyer in Jonas knew that Serena's stipulation made sense. Continuing an intimate relationship would complicate things, and everything was already complicated enough. The last thing Jonas needed— the *very* last thing—was for the bride he'd married in a whirlwind to wind up expecting his child. As it was, they hadn't been exactly careful on their wedding night.

He took a quick pull on his beer. If she were pregnant, or were to become pregnant, no easy way out of their marriage would exist regardless of the election's outcome.

"About that. The other night we didn't use any…um… Is there a possibility that…?" He gulped another swig of beer, but his mouth remained as dry as talc.

"No."

After that highly personal exchange, the

conversation turned decidedly businesslike. They discussed her move to Vegas in strictly utilitarian terms. He would rent an SUV to haul what she needed right away. What didn't fit would either be shipped or remain in her apartment. She'd deal with the issue of subleasing at a later date. He gave her a time to expect him in San Diego on Friday, and promised to email her a copy of his itinerary for the rest of the week, so she could reach him if need be.

"Thanks, Serena," he said again as the conversation wound down.

"Sure."

"See you on Friday."

She laughed nervously. "I'll be waiting."

So much had been settled, Jonas thought. All those pesky Is dotted and Ts crossed. He should have felt relieved that she'd agreed to his plan. But long after he'd hung up one question weighed on his mind: how was he going to live under the same roof as Serena and keep his hands to himself?

CHAPTER FIVE

JONAS had four days and more than three hundred and fifty miles to come up with an answer, but when he pulled the SUV into the parking lot of Serena's apartment building just past noon on Friday he remained stumped.

He was a man known for his control. Serena was the only woman in his experience who'd managed to snap it. He still didn't understand why exactly, even though he'd replayed in his head every minute of their time together. That had given rise to its own set of problems, Jonas thought grimly as he got out of the SUV and stretched. The sky was cloudless and the sun hot as it beat down and bounced off the blacktop. Even so, he knew it wasn't what was responsible for making him uncomfortably warm. Taking a deep breath, he headed inside.

Serena's apartment door was half open, and from his vantage point he could tell she'd been busy. Several boxes and a couple of suit-cases were stacked just inside the entryway. He didn't have a chance to announce his arrival before he heard her demand angrily, "Why did you bother coming?"

That took him aback—until he realized she wasn't speaking to him. She had company.

"To try and talk some sense into you. Not that we've ever succeeded on *that* score," a raspy female voice replied.

"You're nearly thirty years old, Serena Jean. At what point are you going to stop re-belling and start acting like a responsible adult?" This time the speaker was a man.

Her parents, Jonas guessed, and his stomach did a queasy roll. Having already spoken to his own, he knew this wasn't going to be pleasant. Even so, he squared his shoul-ders and stepped into the apartment.

The night they'd met Serena had men-tioned that her father, Buck Warren, was a retired navy man. Jonas had pictured stove-pipe arms, a barrel chest and a fierce expres-sion. He wasn't far off, he realized now. Buck stood just over six feet tall and, while his midsection was nearly wider than his shoul-ders, he had an intimidating presence—thanks in part to twin anchor tattoos on his forearms and steely eyes that glared out from beneath a pair of bushy brows. He transferred his gaze to Jonas the moment he spied him.

"Is this the son of a—?"

"Benjamin," Jonas broke in. "I'm Jonas Benjamin. Serena's husband." It felt odd to say it aloud. He crossed the room and stretched out a hand, which the older man proceeded to crush under the guise of shaking it. Two could play that game. Jonas squeezed right back, and without blinking added, "It's nice to meet you, sir."

Bushy brows shot up. Even so, Buck warned him. "We'll see about that—won't we, son?"

Jonas half expected the man to order him to drop to the floor and give him fifty pushups. Instead Buck crossed his meaty arms and scowled.

"Dad, please," Serena said.

She stood next to the desk in the corner, packing up its contents. She wore a delicate purple blouse whose loose half-sleeves reminded him of a butterfly's wings when she moved. She'd paired it with scandalously short jean cut-offs and silver gladiator sandals. Funky iridescent chandelier earrings dripped nearly to her shoulders. As outfits went it was outrageous and sexy, and unlike anything any of the females of his acquaintance would be caught dead wearing. Yet there it was again—that inexplicable zap of not only attraction but connection.

"Hi."

"Hi." She looked lovely, but exhausted. He understood perfectly. It had been one roller-coaster of a week, and *he* hadn't been the one who'd had to quit his job and pack up his life. She was holding a dagger-like letter opener, which she waved at him, her expression a mixture of embarrassment and surprise. "You're—early."

"Actually, I'm late. I ran into a couple of traffic snarls on Interstate Fifteen," he said.

"Oh, right." She glanced at her wrist, apparently expecting to find a watch there, but it was bare except for a couple of rubber bands. "I guess I'm running a little behind. My parents stopped by unexpectedly." This time she waved the dagger a little more menacingly.

The woman standing next to the open balcony door harrumphed loudly. "You honestly didn't think we were going to let you move to another state with a stranger without trying to talk you out of it, did you?"

"This is my mother Susanne." Serena's smile was brittle as she made the introduction.

Jonas saw similarities between the women. They shared a delicate jaw, an ivory complexion and wide green eyes. But Susanne exhibited none of Serena's vitality and animation. Nor had the years been especially kind to the older woman. Jonas figured Susanne's nicotine habit hadn't helped matters. She was holding a lit cigarette, the smoke forming a cloud around her lined face.

"Hello, ma'am."

This time, instead of being crushed, the hand he offered was met with outright rejection. Susanne took a deep drag of her cigarette instead. In her only bow to courtesy she pursed her lips to one side to exhale the stream of smoke, so that it didn't hit him full in the face. Even so, the insult was as obvious as it was intended.

"God, Mother," Serena muttered. She turned to Jonas. "Let me apologize for their rudeness. As you may have gathered, my parents are not happy with me right now." She laughed without humor. "Actually, they've rarely been happy with me since the day I was born, but at the moment they are especially displeased."

Jonas didn't know what she'd told her parents about her decision to move to Vegas.

They should have discussed this beforehand, he realized. But, whether she'd given the Warrens the straight truth or a more parent-friendly version, the two of them needed to present a united front. He moved closer and put his arm around her.

"No need to apologize. They have every right to be upset with me. Perhaps we could sit down and discuss this." He glanced at Buck and Susanne before letting his gaze return to Serena. The smile he gave her was intended to telegraph support. "That might allay some of their concerns."

"Is she pregnant?" The blunt question, which came from Buck, had Jonas's knees threatening to buckle, even though he and Serena had already nixed that possibility the other night.

Before either of them could answer, Susanne said, "She claims not to be, but as far as I can see the only reason she would have to elope to Vegas with a man she's never mentioned, much less brought around to meet us, would be because she got herself into trouble."

"I'm not pregnant and I didn't elope, Mom. As I explained to you and Dad *twice* already, I met Jonas last weekend when I went to Las Vegas with my friends."

"Some friends," her mother muttered.

"Where were *they* while you were off with a strange man, letting him talk you into making one of the biggest mistakes of your life?"

"This isn't their fault."

"No," her father agreed. "It's yours. You don't think. It's like there's nothing between your ears but that fancy frosting you decorate those silly cakes with."

"Sir," Jonas began. "If I may—"

"I'll get to you in a minute, junior." Buck pointed a thick finger in his direction.

"Junior?" Okay, Serena's father was upset. Jonas got that. Indeed, he accepted responsibility for it. But that didn't mean he would stand for being treated like a teenager who'd brought his date home past curfew.

"Yeah. *Junior,*" Buck sneered. "I've met your sort before. Good-looking, slick-talking preppies with more money than common sense. You're happy to ride through life on Daddy's dime rather than do an honest day's work."

"Dad—" Serena began. To no avail. Buck talked right over her.

"I had your number the moment you walked through the door, wearing your designer label clothes and Hollywood smile. You've probably never done a hard day's work in your life. I worked my way up from Seaman Recruit to Senior Chief Petty Officer during my twenty years serving in the United States Navy. In the meantime snot-nosed rich kids ripe from the academy cake-walked their way to Lieutenant in a fraction of that time."

"Dad, please. Let's not turn this into a dissertation on class."

Buck waved off her second attempt to intervene. He was either oblivious to her mortification or taking delight in it.

"But I still don't get what you want with my daughter. Although she's pretty enough, especially now that her hair's not hot pink or some other unnatural color."

"Don't forget the five eyebrow rings," Susanne inserted on a snort.

Eyebrow rings? Jonas stole a glance in Serena's direction. He couldn't picture anything marring the perfection of those arched brows, much less the sort of piercings about which her mother was talking.

"I only had them for a couple months, when I was twenty-three," Serena muttered on a shrug. "Way too much maintenance for my taste, and not exactly me."

"My point is she's not your type any more than you're hers," Buck finished.

It was true. Jonas's head had told him that from the start. Still…

"Opposites attract, Dad," Serena said. "Look at you and Mom."

Buck grunted. Susanne puffed her cigarette and let out a stream of smoke that apparently served as her reply. Jonas didn't need a psychology degree to figure out that the Warrens were not happy with each other, or with life in general. He felt sorry for them, but sorrier for Serena. His parents were far from perfect. His father in particular could be demanding and overbearing. But they were kindness itself compared to hers.

Still, Jonas felt the need to put their minds at ease. "I have nothing but respect for your daughter—" he began.

"What's really going on here?" the older man demanded.

"Just what I've told you, Dad," Serena inserted. "I've never met anyone like Jonas. Right off the bat, we just…clicked."

Buck's expression said he wasn't buying it. "I can see you getting married on a whim. I sometimes think you have less sense than God gave a gnat. But there's something you're not telling me. Why else would you uproot your life and quit your job for a man you've known less than a week?"

"You thought my job was a waste of time," she shot back. "I believe your exact words were: *'Cake decorating is a hobby, but it's not a career.'* You didn't think I had a future in it."

"Still don't," he barked. "But at least you stuck with it for a few months."

"Eleven."

Buck rubbed a hand over his bristly salt-and-pepper hair and turned his attention to Jonas. "What happens when you tire of her? She's a novelty now, but one look at you and I can see she's not in your league. We both know it."

"Watch it."

Buck's eyes narrowed. "What did you say?"

"I said watch it. You're speaking about my wife." Jonas debated adding *sir*, decided against it. His manners had been stretched to the limit, though he'd kept a rein on his temper. It wouldn't do to lose it now.

"Who do you think you're talking to, son?" Buck demanded, taking a couple of menacing steps forward.

Jonas did the same, till the two men stood toe to toe in the center of the small room.

"I'm not your son. I'm your daughter's husband." That made it twice now that he'd referred to himself as such, and once he'd referred to Serena as his wife. The words settled in and seemed to take hold. "You can call me Jonas, but I don't answer to junior."

Buck eyed him before giving a quick nod. "You've got some spine, I see."

"So does your daughter."

Buck's hand swiped through the air, negating the comment. "Don't mistake her mouth for spine. She does as she pleases, but that doesn't make it the right thing. Well, she's your problem now."

"Is that all you're going to say, Buck?" Susanne crushed the butt of her cigarette into the dirt of a potted plant and stalked forward.

"What more do you expect me to do? She's an adult, even if she never acts like one." Buck motioned toward Jonas. "At least this one's not wearing sandals, can afford to pay the rent and has a decent haircut."

"She said he's some kind of lawyer. My bet is he made her sign one of those agreements before they got married. She's probably going to wind up without a job and without a cent when it's all said and done." Her lips twisted, making the lines that feathered out from them all the more noticeable. "Guess whose problem she'll be then!"

"Stop it! Both of you. Please." Serena's face had gone from beet-red to sheet-white and was now crimson again. "I'm nobody's problem, and I didn't marry Jonas for his money."

"See!" Susanne spat. "It's exactly as I thought. When the newness of being a wife wears off she'll be calling home, asking us to come and bail her out—just like she did when she moved to Los Angeles the summer after high school, thinking she could act." To Jonas, Susanne said, "All she did was wait tables before getting canned."

"I was nineteen then."

"Ten years later you're still going off on a whim," Susanne accused.

From their comments, it was clear Serena hadn't told her parents that she was remaining married to Jonas to save his mayoral candidacy, and in return he was going to help her start a cake-decorating business. He could only imagine the tone of the conversation if she had.

Again he sought to ease the tension.

"Look, Mr. and Mrs. Warren, you don't know me, and I'm sure all of this has come as a shock. Why don't we all sit down and discuss the situation in a calm and rational manner?"

It turned out that calm and rational were foreign concepts to the elder Warrens. They stomped out of the apartment a couple of minutes later—but not before dousing Serena in guilt for being such a disappointment and then disowning her.

Silence, the kind that followed fierce thunderstorms, reigned after their departure. Jonas couldn't believe what had just happened. Serena, however, pulled open another desk drawer and resumed packing.

"God, I'm sorry," he told her. The sentiment, though heartfelt, seemed trite given what had just occurred. He'd turned her life upside down. He hadn't considered how much chaos his plan would cause her, only how much it would benefit him. "Do you want to go after them? Or I could."

She shook her head and continued emptying items into the box.

Jonas inhaled deeply. "Serena, if you want to change your mind about our deal I'll understand." Selfishly, of course, he hoped she wouldn't. But after the scene he'd just witnessed Jonas would have to be an absolute heel not to give her the option.

Her hands stilled and she glanced up. "Thanks, but no."

"Maybe you should take a moment to think about it."

Her expression softened. Jonas wished he could read minds, so that he could know what she was thinking, and then found himself glad that he couldn't when she said simply, "You need me."

True words, he thought, without fully understanding why he felt that way.

"I do." He'd said the very same thing less than a week ago. In both cases he'd felt desperate. But he wasn't without honor. "But I don't want to come between you and your family."

The drawer was empty. The box was full. Serena reached for the packing tape. "Don't worry about it, Jonas."

Her blasé attitude had him gaping. "They just disowned you."

"It's not the first time. It won't be the last. I've never been able to measure up in their eyes. I quit trying a long, long time ago."

She sounded resigned, but beneath her nonchalance Jonas thought he detected pain. He understood its origin. He had a similar old wound that had yet to heal.

"My father considers *me* a disappointment, too."

That got her attention. "You?"

"According to his plan for my life I should already be married, have two-point-five kids and be running for re-election in a statewide race."

"Hey, one out of three isn't bad." She tilted her head to one side and her earrings shimmered. "Of course I'm guessing I'm not the kind of daughter-in-law your dad had in mind."

"No." But Jonas wasn't sure if that was because of Serena's offbeat ways or the fact that her tenure was temporary.

She didn't appear insulted. "You made the grade in my dad's book. Your tidy haircut sealed it, but things were already looking good when your knees didn't buckle the moment he shook your hand."

"The man has a death grip."

She smiled. "You gave as good as you got."

Jonas didn't deny it. "I don't believe in backing down."

"Neither do I." She tore off a large strip of tape and placed it over the box's flaps. "But it stinks that I'm going to have to hear them say *I told you so* when I move back from Vegas after our annulment."

"Not I told you so. You'll have begun your own business," he reminded her.

"That's right." She nodded. "Serenity Cakes."

"You've already come up with a name?"

"I've had a name for a while now," she corrected with a grin.

"I like it."

"Thanks." She dusted her hands together before setting them on her hips. "Well, that's one set of parents down. Now we only have one to go."

"Mine will be easier," he assured her. "They spend most of their time in Washington, although my mother is in Las Vegas right now. And they know all about our arrangement. As does my older sister, Elizabeth."

Jonas expected the news to be met with relief. Serena paled instead. "They do?"

"My campaign manager took it upon himself to relay the information to my father." Jonas wasn't happy with the development, even though he'd planned to do the very same thing—his own way and in his own time. "I don't know if I mentioned it, but my father is a United States Congressman. Jameson wanted to be sure if the story leaked we were all on the same page."

"Jameson sounds very thorough." Her mouth puckered on the word as if it were a sourball.

"Annoyingly so," Jonas agreed. "But it's

his job to be. He's trying to help me win an election."

"I guess that's my new job, too."

Serena helped Jonas load the boxes and her suitcases into the SUV. What didn't fit would be shipped. What she wouldn't need for the next several months would remain in her studio, until she either found someone to sublet it or she returned from Vegas. As for her car—she'd decided to leave it here, too. Molly and Jayne had promised to come over and start it on occasion. Serena held no illusions the old rustbucket could make the trip to Vegas and back without a visit or two to an auto mechanic.

"Is that it?" he asked.

"I guess so."

He settled his hands on his hips and looked around. "Are you set to go, or do you need a few minutes?"

"I'm set. You haven't forgotten about meeting my friends?"

"No. You'll have to tell me how to get to their house."

After Jayne's wedding had been called off, she'd moved into Molly's small bungalow.

"It's not far, and sort of on the way. You'll like them," she added as they got into the vehicle.

"Think they'll like me? I won't blame them for holding a grudge. Because of me you're moving to another state." Half of his mouth crooked up as he put the key in the ignition.

The SUV's six-cylinder revved to life, and so did Serena's hormones. Jonas had a great mouth. It was very expressive. The night they'd met it had been very persuasive.

He turned out of the parking lot onto a road that was busy with midday traffic, through which he maneuvered deftly enough. The afternoon sun lit the gold in his hair. She recalled weaving her fingers through it on their wedding night. It was thick and surprisingly soft to the touch. She knotted her hands together in her lap. These were the wrong things to recall, confined as they were in such a small space.

Serena swallowed and let her gaze detour to his clothes. Despite the heat and manual labor, his khaki trousers and short-sleeved button-down shirt remained crisp. He looked ready for an afternoon on the golf course— while she looked ready for the mosh pit at an alternative music concert.

"My friends aren't holding a grudge. They know the real reason I'm going with you."

Serena needed to remember the real reason, too.

CHAPTER SIX

THEIR visit with Molly and Jayne wasn't long. It lasted barely an hour, during which time the four of them ate a light lunch and made small talk. The meeting wasn't as tension-filled as the one with her parents had been. No accusations were hurled, no insults spoken or implied. But it was awkward—surprisingly so, considering that Serena's friends were privy to the details of her and Jonas's marriage. They knew it was a sham, a union that would continue in name only, and only as long as necessary to guarantee Jonas's political future.

That was why Serena didn't understand the curious glances she kept intercepting. They made her wonder if Molly and Jayne were reading too much into the fact that Jonas had opened the SUV's door for her and taken the seat next to her on the sofa while a nearby chair went unoccupied.

Still, they were courteous with their questions, probing only just enough to make it clear they were looking out for Serena's best interests. She loved them all the more for it after her own parents had washed their hands of her…again.

When Jonas excused himself to use the bathroom, just before they were leaving, Molly and Jayne turned their questions to Serena.

"Okay, spill," Molly said as they stood in the small foyer. "There's more than *convenience* to this marriage, isn't there?"

"Why do you say that?"

Molly tucked a handful of dark hair behind one ear. "Because it's like the night at the Bellagio all over again. The air practically sizzles between the pair of you."

"I've got to agree." Jayne looked worried.

"That's just attraction. It's natural. We went over this the other night. He's sexy and gorgeous." At their raised eyebrows, Serena added, "It means nothing."

"Yeah, well, don't discount attraction. It can make you do extremely foolish things," Molly said.

"As if I need reminding."

"I'm not talking about you." Molly's expression was rueful as she plucked at the knee of her Capri pants.

Before Serena could ask what she meant, though, Jayne was saying, "Are you sure you're doing this for the right reasons, Serena? I know we made that list of the pros and cons, and staying married for the interim seemed to make sense. But I'm worried about you, honey. You're going to be so far away."

Serena swallowed the lump in her throat. "Alex will be there."

"I know, but I don't want to see you get your heart broken."

As Jayne's had been.

Serena wrapped her friend in a fierce hug. "No need to worry on that score. Jonas and I aren't in love or anything like that."

She'd intended the words to be reassuring, but now she was the one plagued with doubts. Love…Serena hadn't figured she'd ever fall for a man or make any kind of commitment. She'd never given herself the chance to, always ending things long before they could start. It had proved an effective strategy…until Vegas and Jonas. What made him different?

The man in question returned then.

"All set?" he asked.

"Yes." The smile Serena beamed was for her friends' benefit.

"Try not to worry," he told Jayne and Molly as he held open the door for Serena. "I'll be good to her."

"See that you are," Molly replied, her tone and demeanor surprisingly threatening for a kindergarten teacher.

He wasn't put off. Rather he took the remark in his stride.

"You're welcome to come and visit any time. My condo has a guest room." Color suffused his cheeks. "Which, of course, you'll have to share with Serena. I'll show you a different side of Vegas. It's a fun town, but there's more to it than casinos, showgirls and blinking neon lights."

It was the blinking neon lights Serena saw when she woke in the SUV's passenger seat just before midnight. Her neck was stiff and the rest of her body didn't feel much better after the long drive. They'd stopped just outside San Bernadino for dinner. Other than one quick bathroom break afterward, they'd driven straight through, and she'd slept the last leg of it.

"We'll be at my apartment in about twenty minutes," Jonas said, reading her mind.

She kneaded her neck and mumbled, "Sorry I've been such poor company."

"That's all right. You needed the sleep. It's been a pretty crazy week."

"Understatement," she replied quietly.

"Yeah."

"You mentioned you live in a condo? Two bedrooms?" Please, God, let the rest of it be bigger than her apartment. If they had to live together her sanity demanded she have more room and privacy than what her studio afforded.

"That's right. It's in a renovated highrise downtown, not far from the Fremont Street Experience." Serena nodded, though she wasn't sure what he was talking about. "I bought it just out of law school, mostly as an investment, using the trust fund I received from my grandparents. I figured I'd eventually buy a house in one of the neighborhoods and sublet the place." He turned and smiled at her. "But I love living there. With all of the redevelopment that's going on in the area there's so much to do. A slew of great shops and restaurants are within walking distance. My office isn't far either."

"It sounds nice." It really did. She liked being in the thick of things.

"I think you'll like it."

"I'm sure I will." She laughed dryly. "You saw the shoebox I called home. I'm pretty easy to please."

"Did you live there long?" he asked conversationally.

These were the kinds of questions singles asked of one another to determine common ground. She and Jonas were bound to one another legally, but to all intents and purposes they'd only gone out on one date. Granted, it had ended in marriage, but... Would he like the fleshed-out version of Serena Warren? He'd met her dysfunctional parents and hadn't run away screaming. But then he couldn't afford to be too judgmental or choosy at this point. He needed Serena.

"I've lived there long for me."

"And that would be?"

"Nearly three years." Normally she wasn't one to volunteer personal information—or any information, really—to the men she dated. An enigma—that was what she preferred to be. But, just as she had the previous Saturday night, Serena found herself opening up and the words pouring out. "I lived in a bigger place before that, but I shared it with another girl and her boyfriend. They were in an alternative band."

"Is that where the inspiration for the eyebrow rings came from?" He smiled.

"No. I'd already given up my piercings by then." She ran a hand idly over her right eyebrow and admitted, "It was a short-lived fad, and not a terribly flattering one."

He sent her a sideways glance. "What about the pink hair? Is that when you had it?"

"Actually, that was prior to pink. I'm pretty sure it was still blue at that point."

"Blue?" His gaze shot back to her.

Serena decided she might as well put it all out there. Their odd and instantaneous attraction aside, Jonas had already figured out how absolutely wrong they were for each other.

"I think I went through every color of the rainbow one at a time. My parents hated it." She shrugged, and could admit it now, "That was part of the appeal."

"What about your friends?" he asked. "I'm having a hard time picturing either Molly or Jayne with a wild dye job. So what did they think?"

Serena's laughter was genuine, and laced with fondness. The women were from differ-

ent walks of life, with vastly different person-
alities. Despite that, when they'd met via a
bookclub five years earlier, they'd all just
clicked. So much so that after the bookclub
broke up their friendship had remained. One
thing Serena knew for certain: she could
count on them.

"Molly was the most shocked. She tends
to be the least spontaneous of us. But, as
strange as they must have found my choices
in hair color, they always helped me touch
up my roots."

Jonas reached over and gave the ends of
her curls a playful tug. As he pulled back his
hand his fingers skimmed her shoulder. The
simple touch was akin to striking a match.
Heat flared instantly.

"I like the color it is now."

"This is the real me." She felt oddly naked
when she said it, as if she were talking about
more than her hair. To be clear for both of them,
she added, "No root touch-ups required."

"I like the real you." He said it lightly.

She matched his tone. "You don't know
the real me."

"No?"

"We're practically strangers, Jonas,
marriage certificate notwithstanding."

His shoulders lifted. "Well, how about this, then? I like what I know."

Ditto, Serena thought. She liked it a little too much for her peace of mind.

"Which hair color was your favorite?" he wanted to know.

Serena was grateful to return to the topic of her tresses. "Out of all the crazy ones, you mean?"

"Yeah."

"Violet." She grinned at the memory of Molly's mouth dropping open when she saw it for the first time. Serena had debuted it the weekend before Easter two years earlier. "My hair was as short as yours, and I wore it spiky on top."

They were stopped at a light, and he studied her as if trying to picture it. The way his brows beetled together spoke volumes about how much Serena had changed since then, even if she was still far from conservative. "No way."

"Yes way."

As his laughter ebbed, she asked, "What would happen if the media got hold of a picture of me from back in the day?"

She'd expected Jonas to sober, but he was still grinning when he said, "I'm less worried about the media than my mother."

"You've never brought someone like me home before, I'm sure."

He did sober somewhat at that. "No. I haven't. Of course I've never brought home a wife either." Before things could get awkward, he winked. "As for the media—maybe I'll leak them one. Vegas is a pretty unconventional town, despite what my campaign manager thinks. I'd have the rebel vote sewn up for sure."

He was joking, of course. If Vegas were so unconventional, Jonas wouldn't have to fake a real marriage to a woman he barely knew and otherwise would have had happily annulled. But he was right on with the rebel comment. The funky hair color choices had been a form of rebellion. Even as her friends had helped Serena apply the dye they'd known that. They'd helped her see it, too. First by accepting her for who she was—something her parents couldn't or wouldn't—and later by helping her to accept herself.

"You're quiet," Jonas said, pulling Serena from her thoughts.

"Just thinking about my friends."

"You know, I meant it when I said they're welcome any time."

"I know. Thanks."

"I want you to be happy, Serena."

She wanted to be happy, too. But as Jonas pulled the SUV into the basement parking structure of his highrise the only thing Serena felt was nervous, and a little sick to her stomach.

"Which bags will you need for tonight?" he asked as they got out and walked to the rear of the vehicle. "I thought we could leave the rest of the unpacking till the morning, if that's okay with you?"

"Sure." She glanced past him into the interior of the SUV. She was in no hurry to unpack and sort through her belongings tonight. "That small one has my toiletries and…um…I think I have some pajamas in the black one with the hot pink ribbon tied to the handle."

She'd marked it for her flight to Vegas, to make it easier to spot on the airport's luggage carousel. Had that really been only a week ago?

He hauled out both, locked the vehicle, and they started for the elevator. She swore it took forever to reach the seventeenth floor. Then everything seemed to happen too fast as they made their way down the well-lit hallway.

Jonas set down the larger bag so he could

unlock the door. After opening it, he pushed it wide.

"Well, this is it."

No lamps illuminated the inside, but the large windows on the far wall let in a neon-tinged glow of light from downtown's signage. Serena took a step forward, only to be stopped when Jonas dropped the toiletries bag to the floor and reached for her arm.

"Wait!"

"Wh—what?"

His expression turned thoughtful. "Shouldn't I…?"

"Shouldn't you what?"

Whatever debate he was having with himself was decided. "Yeah. I should."

Having said so, Jonas offered a smile that sent Serena's hormones into a tailspin. She had no time to pull them out of it before he swept her up in his arms and stepped across the threshold.

"Welcome to your new home, Mrs. Benjamin." His smile faltered then. She might have thought it was because of his words, but she knew better when his gaze dipped to her lips.

Don't kiss me, she pleaded silently, only to be sorely disappointed when he didn't. He set her on her feet and released her, stepping a good three feet away afterward.

"Sorry." He tucked his hands into his pockets. "I guess I got carried away."

That seemed to happen whenever they were together, Serena thought. One or both of them acted on impulse.

Jonas was saying, "It's just that it's tradition for the groom to carry his bride over the threshold…"

"And you're a traditional kind of guy?"

He nodded.

Serena wasn't traditional. Nor was their marriage. "Now is probably a good time to mention that I've decided not to change my last name."

"Oh?"

"It would be a real hassle to change everything back afterward," she pointed out.

"I suppose so." He worked up a smile—the kind that any politician worth his salt could manufacture when the situation called for it. "Well, *Ms. Warren*, welcome home anyway."

Home. That made it twice he'd referred to his condo as that. The word poked at her heart, but she wouldn't allow it to penetrate. This wasn't the real thing—any more than those naval-base apartments she'd lived in growing up had been. Home was a place of permanence and security. It was where families gathered for dinners that were not punctuated with yelling and arguments. Where parents offered praise and encouragement instead of constant criticism. Where husbands and wives hadn't already determined how and when their marriage would end. In other words it was a place that didn't exist. At least not for someone like Serena.

"Can you show me to my room?" she asked politely.

He frowned. "I get the feeling I've offended you somehow."

She started to shake her head, but then decided to be honest. "You haven't offended me, but we need to be clear. This isn't my home, Jonas."

"No, but for the time being—"

"For the time being I'm *pretending* to be your wife." If the words were spoken a little harshly, she wouldn't regret that. They both needed to remember what was and wasn't real. Neither of them could afford to get caught up in the fairytale they'd succumbed to a week earlier.

"Right. I just thought…" A muscle ticked in his jaw. "Sorry."

He turned away to retrieve her bags from the hall and then closed the door. Thankfully no one had witnessed the exchange. Serena could only imagine what another tenant would make of the coolly pragmatic conversation that had followed Jonas's romantic gesture.

Jonas turned back to her. Already he had transformed from solicitous groom to impersonal tour guide. "Well, this is…*my* home— seventeen hundred square feet of usable living space."

The foyer opened into a tastefully decorated living room that looked like something straight out of a magazine. Restrained touches of olive and rusty red were found in the accent pillows that lined a gold chenille sofa. The colors complemented two oversized paintings of the Tuscan countryside that hung in the room. Everything was coordinated. It was the complete opposite of the mix-and-match collection of furniture and styles that had populated Serena's tiny studio. But at least her furniture told a story. It reflected who she was. Other than the large flat-screen television that was mounted over the fireplace, Jonas's decor did little to fill in any of the blanks she had about the man. Nor did it do anything to dispel her notion of him as ultra-conservative.

Because he seemed to be waiting for her to say something, she told him, "It's very clean."

"I have a housekeeper. Mrs. Danielson. She comes in once a week. But I'm not a slob." As if to underscore the point, he retrieved his keys from where he'd dropped them on the foyer's console table and stowed them in one of its drawers.

A place for everything, and everything in its place.

Where was Serena's place? Twenty-nine years old and she still didn't know.

"The kitchen is that way." Jonas pointed to the right.

Beyond a wide archway was a dining room table with enough dark wood chairs to seat six. She assumed the kitchen he spoke of was through the door just beyond.

"Miss Danielson does the grocery shopping when my schedule is especially tight."

"I'm happy to take over that job while I'm here." The devil made Serena add, "You like tofu, right?"

"I'm always game to try new things," he replied seriously.

His gaze was back on her mouth, dredging

up memories of their wedding night that were best left buried.

"We should go to bed," Serena said. She felt her cheeks heat. She cleared her throat. "I mean, I'm really tired."

He nodded slowly. "You're welcome to either bedroom. But the master is a little larger, and has more closet space. Plus it has its own bathroom."

Serena couldn't imagine sleeping in Jonas's bed. Unless he was in there with her. "The guest room is fine," she answered hastily. "No sense making you move your belongings when mine are already boxed up and waiting to be unpacked."

"Are you sure? The mattress on my bed is better quality—much firmer." This time he was the one who flushed.

"I've slept on a pull-down bed for nearly three years," she reminded him. "I'm sure the mattress in your guestroom will be a huge step up."

He lifted her bags again, and started down the hall. The first door on the left revealed an office full of dark wood and masculine hues. A massive desk faced the door. It was so tidy, with "in" and "out" boxes clearly labeled, and nary a paperclip out of place. What a stark contrast to the one that had been all but hidden beneath papers and clutter in the corner of her studio.

The guest bath was across from the office. He set her toiletries bag inside and showed her how to work the shower. She tried to pay attention, but got distracted watching his shirt pull across his shoulders.

"You turn it like this to regulate the temperature."

If only it were so easy, she thought.

Next to the guest bath was the master suite. It was outfitted with a huge platform bed. The mattress beneath the crisp chocolate and robin-egg duvet did indeed look firm, not to mention inviting.

Because Serena could easily picture herself there, and not alone, she turned away.

"Here you go." Jonas held open the door to the room directly across the hall from his.

It was smaller than the master, but far bigger than what she was used to. She took in the queen-sized sleigh bed, dresser and armoire. Very tasteful, and all the pieces matched. But she couldn't help thinking the room was bland. From the walls to the bedding to the window treatments and carpet everything was in varying shades of beige.

Serena was so *not* beige, but she plastered a smile on her face and told him, "It's very nice."

Jonas surprised her by laughing. "You're such a liar. You don't like it."

She decided not to argue the point. "That obvious?"

Jonas shrugged. "Afraid so. It would be even if I hadn't been to your apartment. You like color. A lot of it."

She found it easy to smile at his assessment. "Yes, I do. In my home and on my clothes."

"On your person, too."

"No more wild hair for me," she reminded him.

His voice lowered. "Actually, I was thinking about that dragonfly tattoo on your hip."

Now Serena was, too, and recalling the way he'd traced its delicate wings with his tongue. They both sobered. Jonas cleared his throat and backed out of the room.

"Well, that's everything. I should let you…" His gaze flicked to the bed and she saw him swallow.

"Yeah. I'm tired. You're probably tired, too."

"Exhausted," he agreed.

He didn't look exhausted. He looked aroused.

"Well, then, I'll see you in the morning."

He nodded. "In the morning."

But he didn't move. Serena forced herself to reach for the door. When it closed Jonas was still standing in the hall.

Jonas paced the length of his bedroom. Despite his claim of being exhausted he was wide awake. Wide awake and frustrated— sexually and otherwise. He was no closer to understanding this insane attraction he felt for Serena. More troubling by far, though, was the fact that he was no closer to being able to control it. It was like a wildfire. Surprising and unpredictable, it burned at will. Right now he felt scorched.

CHAPTER SEVEN

MUSIC woke Jonas the next morning. It wasn't soft or soothing, but pulsating and loud—the hard rock equivalent of the military's reveille. It blasted in all its static glory from the direction of the guest room for a full sixty seconds before finally shutting off. The silence that followed was punctuated by footsteps and muttering.

Serena.

It was just after seven o'clock on a Saturday morning. Apparently his wife was an early riser.

Jonas got out of bed and hurriedly pulled on the same clothes he'd worn the day before. When he opened the bedroom door Serena was just coming out of her room across the hall. Her eyes were heavy with sleep, her hair a sexy rumpled mess. She was wearing plaid boxer shorts and a wrinkled white tee-shirt that sported the silhouette of a bronco rider. She might as well have been wearing clingy lingerie the way his body responded upon seeing her. He was glad he'd left his shirt untucked. The tails offered some camouflage for his condition.

"Good morning," he managed at last.

She crossed her arms over her chest, the gesture born of modesty rather than defensiveness, and mumbled, "Sorry if I woke you. My clock has a battery backup and I never turned off the alarm when I packed it. I had to shove through a couple of boxes to find it."

Jonas smiled. "I would have gotten up eventually anyway." Like in two or four hours, given the fact he hadn't fallen asleep until well after two a.m.

"Well, I was just on my way to the…" She pointed in the direction of the bathroom.

"Right. I'll start the coffee."

They both stepped into the hallway at the same time, nearly colliding.

"Sorry." The apologies were issued simultaneously.

"This is awkward," Serena said.

"I know." He shoved a hand through his hair as he exhaled.

"I'm sure it will get easier," she offered. "It's just a new routine for both of us to get used to."

As Jonas watched her disappear into the bathroom, he was sure of no such thing.

They met up in the kitchen half an hour later. Serena was fresh from a shower and dressed. Unfortunately for Jonas he found her outfit to be no less sexy than her sleep-wear. He liked just a little too much the way the ruffled detail that ran down the front of her white blouse drew attention to her breasts. And while her embroidered shorts were a re-spectable length they left enough of her toned thighs exposed to turn his breathing labored.

"Coffee's ready." The words came out reedy. If she noticed, she didn't comment. Instead, she was looking around.

His kitchen was small, though maple cabi-netry with glass inserts helped to make it seem larger. It didn't have room for a proper table, since it was adjacent to the dining room, but the breakfast bar, which seated two, was perfect for his needs. Jonas ate most of his meals there, and even though he had a computer on the desk in his office he tended to read his email on his laptop, seated on one of the tall stools.

The breakfast bar was in front of a window

that offered an excellent view of the downtown area, including the revitalized Fremont Street. Even at this early hour it had a similar energy level to that of the Strip. It was one of the things he loved about living here. One of the things Jonas loved about Las Vegas in general.

"This is a nice room. Great appliances. Do you enjoy cooking?"

A laugh escaped before he admitted, "I can't boil water."

"Oh."

"I assume you know your way around a kitchen?" he replied.

Serena shook her head. Damp curls bobbed invitingly, and some of her sass was back when she said, "You assume wrong, Counselor. I can bake, and of course I can decorate a cake, but I'm not much of a chef."

"What about the tofu you offered to make last night?" he teased.

She grinned. "I lied. Not only can't I cook the stuff, I don't like it."

"I guess that means we'll be eating a lot of takeout."

"Oh, I don't know. I can manage a couple dishes. I've mastered omelets, for instance." She crossed to the refrigerator. Opening the door, she said, "Let's see what you've got to work with."

Though he knew it was a risk, Jonas walked over to peer inside with her. While the scents of soap and citrus flooded his senses, Serena was busy plucking a bell pepper and a green onion from the crisper. She snatched up the carton of eggs next.

His stomach growled loudly and she laughed.

"Someone's hungry." She sobered when their gazes met.

So much for thinking he'd been successful in hiding his interest. "Serena—"

She stepped around him before he could figure out what to say. "Grab the milk and shredded cheddar, okay?"

While she chopped the vegetables, and whisked the eggs and milk together, he set out plates and silverware and poured them each a cup of coffee. To an outside observer the scene was one of domestic harmony. For Jonas it was an absolute nightmare. He felt ready to explode.

He'd spent lazy weekend mornings with a woman before. In his kitchen and in his bed. Janet had stayed over so often during their years as a couple that she'd had her own key.

But his ex hadn't been much of a cook either. She'd grown up wealthy and pampered and, like Jonas, had continued to hire out most of the household chores. When they'd eaten breakfast in it had been cold cereal, or a couple of slices of toast while they shared sections of the newspaper in companionable silence. She'd never puttered in front of his stove with a dishtowel tucked around her waist, looking as delicious as a gourmet meal.

Serena glanced over her shoulder at him then. "I know what you're thinking."

He nearly choked on his coffee. "You do?"

"I added too much cheese."

"Uh…"

"You can never have too much cheese. I think it's an unwritten rule. Besides, cheese is loaded with calcium. Good for your bones."

He wasn't worried about his bones, but he nodded. "Anything you need me to do?"

"Nah. I've got it all under control."

It was just after Serena made that assurance that the smoke alarm went off. Its high-pitched squeal rent the early-morning quiet just as effectively as her clock radio had. They both rushed to the far counter, where smoke spiraled up from one side of the toaster. While she tried to jemmy free a stuck piece of burned toast, Jonas grabbed the dish-towel from her waist and began frantically fanning the air just below the detector. It seemed to take forever before it quit. When it did, they looked at one another and burst out laughing.

"Way to go, Red."

"I'd better get back to the eggs before I burn them, too." She nodded to the blackened bread. "I'll leave this in your capable hands."

He stopped her before she could turn away. "Wait. You forgot your apron."

Jonas didn't hand her the dishtowel. He put it around her waist and tucked the ends into the band of her shorts in the back. His hands settled there afterward, not quite holding her. Even so, she didn't move. Slowly she brought her gaze up. Slowly he tilted his chin down. She rose on tiptoe. He held his breath. Her arms came up, rested on his shoulders. Jonas closed the last bit of distance between their mouths. The kiss lasted until the smoke alarm blared a second time. The kitchen reeked of burnt eggs and cheese. The omelet was unsalvageable. They wound up forgoing breakfast and making do with just coffee, but as the day wore on Jonas knew that wasn't why he felt so damned famished.

* * *

Serena was putting away the last of her clothes when Jonas knocked at the door to the guest room. She'd closeted herself inside with the boxes Jonas had brought up from the SUV just after their aborted meal. She'd needed to regain her equilibrium. Their kiss had knocked her off her foundation. No matter how many times she reminded herself that she needed to keep her distance, she found herself drawn to Jonas—a moth to the flame...and certain doom. Even if she were the sort of woman who believed in happily ever after, he'd already made it clear their relationship was temporary, and that was what she had agreed to as well.

"Come in," she called.

Jonas opened the door, but remained in the hallway. His expression was wary—and no wonder, given the earlier fireworks. Still, if he'd come to apologize—

"About what happened in the kitchen...I just wanted to say I'm sorry."

Damn him! Serena opened a small box and began untangling pairs of earrings. "Forget about it," she muttered.

"You're mad."

"I said forget about it." She took the box to the dresser, presenting him with her back. Not that it mattered. She could see him clearly in the mirror.

"You also made me promise this would be a marriage in name only." He motioned with one hand. "I…I got carried away."

"I was there, Jonas. You didn't get carried away all by yourself."

His gaze sharpened. He was every inch the lawyer when he asked, "Is that why you're mad?"

"Look, I'm not going to pretend I'm not attracted to you, Jonas. You know I am. That's why we're in the predicament we're in."

"Is it the only reason we're in this predicament?"

"You tell me?" she demanded as she turned.

"I…I…"

He was off balance. Well, welcome to the club, she thought. Serena pressed her advantage. "Why did you want to marry me? The night we met you said you wanted me to stay with you, but why marriage?"

"I've asked myself that same question," he admitted. "I've also wondered why you said yes."

She remained silent now.

Jonas sighed. "Look, I didn't come in here to pick a fight."

"No, you came to apologize."

He ignored her tone. "And to give you this."

Jonas stepped into the room and held out his hand. Cradled in his palm was a small leather box. Serena knew what she would find inside before she opened it. The platinum wedding band was accompanied by a brilliant-cut solitaire diamond that was big enough to have cost a small fortune. But it was the irony of the timing that had her gasping. They had no explanation other than moonlight and madness for why they'd gotten married in the first place, yet here he was presenting her with a rock and a band that were supposed to symbolize his undying devotion.

Of course the rings were just a prop, she reminded herself. His constituents would expect the wife of the candidate to be wearing them. Despite the stab of disappointment she felt, Serena decided it was a good thing no real meaning was attached to them. After all, they were *so* not her taste.

That must have occurred to Jonas then, too. "My sister picked out the set."

His sister. Though Serena had yet to meet

Elizabeth, she pictured a woman who would be at home in a country club or standing on the deck of a yacht. Long straight hair, thick headband, tasteful designer clothes.

"The rings are nice." Nice and traditional.

"Try them on," he suggested.

The band slid over her knuckle with ease—a little big, but not too bad. When she slipped on the other ring, though, the heavy stone listed to one side.

"I guess it has to be resized." He sighed. "I was hoping you could wear it tonight."

Ah, yes, tonight's fund-raising dinner, at which time Serena would be introduced to the public as his wife. Jonas had explained the plan during yesterday's long drive, as well as the rationale behind it. His campaign manager felt that calling a press conference to announce their marriage would invite too much speculation. This would make it less of a big deal.

"I have an idea." Serena went to her jewelry box and returned with a rectangular bauble that was intended to pass for blue topaz surrounded by diamonds and set in white gold. Nothing about it was pricey, let alone semi-precious. She'd bought it off a department store shelf for the bargain price of forty percent off retail a couple of months back. The main stone was bigger than the real diamond, and the ring eclipsed the delicately etched platinum wedding band. They didn't go together at all, which in her book made them perfect. Serena smiled. "This is more me."

Jonas stared at her in thoughtful silence before nodding.

She handed him back the pricey diamond, which he tucked in his pocket. "That reminds me. I have something of yours." He coughed as he backed into the hall. "A couple of things, actually."

He was back a moment later. "I found this on the floor next to the nightstand in our hotel room."

It was one of the earrings she'd worn the night they'd met.

"Thanks. They're my favorite pair. I'd given it up as lost for good."

"I also…um…found this." He held out his other hand, revealing crumpled lavender satin and lace.

It was her bra. Jonas had helped her out of it on their wedding night. Desire had made his hands clumsy and the act all the more endearing. Recalling it now sent heat spiraling through her. Her hands were the clumsy ones now as she took it from him. To keep from humiliating herself Serena quipped, "Gee, I feel a little bit like Cinderella. Which one should I try on for you first?"

Joke or not, it was the wrong thing to ask. Jonas's eyes darkened. "I get a choice?"

"I...I..." It was her turn to stammer helplessly.

He saved her from answering. "So, what do you plan to wear tonight?"

"Worried I'll embarrass you?" Though she said it lightly, Serena held her breath as she awaited his answer.

"Just wondering which tie I should wear."

"Men have such easy choices," she complained on an airy sigh as she crossed to the closet.

It was a walk-in number, with shelves and racks that lined three of its walls. Though Serena considered herself a bit of a clothes-horse, she had managed to fill up barely half of it. Even to her eyes the assortment of vivid colors and wild patterns made for a garish display. One look at his face and she knew he was concerned.

"So, what's the dress code?" she asked.

"Nothing too fancy."

"You're wearing a suit," she reminded him.

"Cocktail casual, then," he amended, as if the description helped clarify things.

"Cocktail casual?" she repeated.

"A dress is fine." He stepped into the closet with her and picked up one leopard-print high heel. Fingering its lethal three-inch spike, he added, "Something in a muted solid color would be best."

Serena worried her lower lip. That left out the sleeveless number that was covered in purple and red geometric shapes, as well as the pumpkin-orange cotton sheath. The cocoa jersey dress might work, except it was cut a little low, and nothing about her little black dress could be considered appropriate for primetime.

As she flipped through the hangers she watched Jonas's thoughtful expression turn into a frown. He cleared his throat. "What would you wear to meet your friends for dinner?"

"Depends on the place, but most of the time I'd wear blue jeans or a miniskirt."

"A miniskirt." His mouth went slack, she presumed in horror.

Serena ushered him out of the closet. "Don't worry about it. I'll figure something out."

Alone, she did a second inventory of her

clothes. Not everything was there yet. Some of the things she didn't wear often were being shipped from San Diego. But it really didn't matter. The sad fact was nothing in her wardrobe said "wife of the candidate." She nibbled her nail. Most of it didn't say wife of any sort, at least not the sort of wife a man like Jonas would have, and that meant she didn't have anything acceptable to wear tonight.

She debated only a moment before snatching up her cellphone and punching in the number that Alex had given her. Serena was grateful beyond measure when her friend answered on the second ring.

"Hi, Alex. Thank God you're there."

"Serena? Are you in Vegas?" Alex asked.

"I'm here." She paced to the window. Outside it was sunny, and probably already scorching hot. "I'm desperate, Alex."

That got her friend's attention. "Desperate? Give me an address and I'll be there to get you before you hang up."

She would be, too. Alex would drop everything to help. That was the kind of friend she was.

"Thanks," Serena murmured, touched and humbled. "But you don't need to rush to my rescue this very minute, or even at all. I'm sorry for being so dramatic. This isn't a matter of life or death." She pressed a hand to her stomach. Though it sort of felt like it.

"So, what's the problem?"

"Jonas has a campaign function I will be attending with him tonight. The Las Vegas Citizens for Change," she enunciated with a stiff accent.

"Sounds dry," Alex commiserated.

"Probably," she agreed, though Serena found herself oddly curious about the grass-roots group of young urban professionals who called the city home and wanted an administration that would cater to their needs as much as it catered to the needs of the business community. "He's going to announce our marriage—introduce me to the masses, so to speak. It will be all over the news after tonight." Picturing herself in a roomful of suit-clad men and demurely dressed women, Serena collapsed onto the mattress and flung a hand over her eyes. "I'm having a fashion emergency."

Her admission was greeted with silence and then laughter. "Don't worry. I've got a few hours when I can slip free this afternoon. We'll go shopping," Alex promised.

* * *

A miniskirt!

Jonas stood under the cool spray of his shower. God help him, he could picture a little too clearly Serena wearing some thigh-baring number. In his fantasy she paired it with the dangly earrings whose mate he'd just returned, the lavender bra, and those sexy leopard-print stilettos.

He groaned, and even after he turned the nozzle all the way to cold his body remained on fire.

Between the kiss in the kitchen and the fantasy image of a miniskirt-wearing Serena dogging his libido, Jonas was in a foul mood when the woman in question tapped at his bedroom door half an hour later.

"I'm heading out," she informed him. "My friend Alex and I are going shopping."

"Now?" He glanced at his wristwatch. Women, he knew, could turn a routine trip to the mall into an all-day excursion. "We need to leave for the dinner no later than four o'clock. Jameson wants us there early, so he can meet you and go over what's expected."

"I won't be gone long."

"Can't it wait till tomorrow?" he asked.

"No. I need to pick out something for tonight." She batted her eyelashes. "It seems that all of my 'cocktail casual' garments are at the cleaners."

The mention of clothing caused Jonas to recall his fantasy, and his libido was teased back to life.

"Just make sure it covers your butt and hits somewhere around the knee," he snapped in frustration.

Her expression sobered at his surly tone and insulting words. He wanted to apologize, maybe even try to explain, but she was gone before he could.

Jonas's parting barb stung. A lot. Serena might not be conventional, but she *had* agreed to help him. She understood what was at stake between now and the election, which was why she was leafing through rack after rack of dresses, looking for something appropriate to wear.

Unfortunately two hours of shopping had yielded only a closet full of options for the real Serena. For the Serena who was the wife of a burgeoning politician the haul included only one very staid taupe suit and some equally bland accessories.

Even Alex was surprised by Serena's choices. "Pearls, hmm? And that suit? Taupe." Her lips wobbled into a smile.

"So?"

Alex swallowed. "Don't get me wrong, honey. It's nice. But it's a bit…boring. Especially for you."

Serena agreed, but she shrugged at the description. "Then Jonas will consider it perfect."

"Are you sure about that? I mean, he fell in lo—" Alex's face colored.

"He fell in lust with me," Serena finished. The blunt word caused a surprisingly sharp pain in her chest.

"He married you."

"But he doesn't have a clue why," she replied, recalling their earlier conversation. On a sigh, she admitted, "Neither of us does."

"But there *was* a reason, Serena. And it wasn't lust. Maybe the two of you just need a little time to figure out what it was."

Alex squeezed her hand and Serena's defenses collapsed. "I'm so not what he wants in a wife—even in a pretend wife. He's afraid I'll embarrass him tonight."

"Did he say that?"

"Not in so many words. But he instructed me to buy something that—and I quote—covers my butt and hits somewhere around the knee."

Alex offered a commiserating smile. "Well, if that's his only criteria this outfit fills the bill."

"Perfectly."

Serena fingered the strand of pearls. She could do this. But maybe there was more than one way to do it, she decided as her rebel instincts kicked in.

Her mood lifted along with her lips as she told Alex, "You know, now that I think of it, I saw something in the last store that would fit the bill, too."

CHAPTER EIGHT

JONAS yanked free his tie and reworked the knot for the third time. Serena had returned from shopping an hour ago, with a large bag in one hand and a huge grin on her face. Both made him nervous.

"Did you find something?" he'd asked.

"I sure did. You'll be pleased, too." She'd sent him a wink. "It covers my butt."

With that she'd disappeared into her room. The only time Jonas had seen her since then was when she'd sauntered out of the steamy guest bath wearing a towel. It had covered her butt, too, but not much else.

"Just about ready, Serena?" he called, stopping in front of her door.

"Almost." A moment later she stepped out of the bedroom, clutching vivid green fabric to her breasts. "If you don't mind, I need a little help."

With that she presented him with her back, where the dress gaped open and revealed the clasp of a black bra. Far lower he spied the flirty top band of a thong in the same hue.

God help him. He still hadn't recovered from seeing her in a towel.

"Jonas?" She glanced over her shoulder at him. "Is the zipper stuck?"

"It works," he muttered. A lot of things were working at that moment.

He zipped the dress, torturing himself by letting his knuckles trail over her soft skin on the way up. When he'd finished, Serena turned. He should have been prepared for the effect she would have on him, but his resistance was low at the moment. The sleeveless silk dress was apple-green, with loose layers that ruffled slightly around her slim hips before falling to just above her knees. A black belt, dotted with rhinestones, accentuated her slim waist, and the peeptoe heels on her feet allowed a glimpse of a more colorful take on a French manicure. Her gemstone necklace matched her earrings. Both were chunky and bold.

His mouth went dry, and the alarm bells that sounded in his head didn't have a lick to do with what Jameson would think. No other woman could have pulled off such an outfit, but Serena was a vision. So much so that Jonas couldn't speak.

"It's not what you had in mind, I know." Her words came out crisp and made it apparent that she'd mistaken the reason for his silence. "And I know we have a deal. I'll try to hold up my end of it, but this is as sedate as it gets. You won't catch me dead in granny pearls and boring taupe." She notched up her chin. "Sorry."

Granny pearls and boring taupe? He wasn't sure what she meant by that. She stuffed something into his hand then.

"I picked this up for you. It's kind of a payback." She cleared her throat. "I mean for the ones I've ruined."

The silk tie was a blinding kaleidoscope of colors. The same shade of green as her dress featured prominently. Jonas had never owned anything remotely like it. The one he had on was deep red with simple black stripes.

"I don't expect you to wear it—tonight or ever. But I thought it was fun." She shrugged and started down the hall.

Jonas tucked the tie into his pocket and followed after her. It wasn't until they were seated in his car that he recovered the power of speech. Even then he only felt prepared to broach a safe subject.

"The group I'm speaking to tonight will be making an endorsement later in the week based in part on what my opponent and I say."

"I know this an important event for you, Jonas. I'll do my part." She fiddled with the hem of her skirt as she stared out her window.

He stared at her bare knees. When he finally returned his gaze to the road he had to jam on the brakes of his car to stop in time for a red light. After the light turned green, he shifted from first to second gear. Even though Jonas always drove within the speed limit, with Serena seated on the passenger side he was tempted to take the highway out to the desert and allow the engine full throttle.

"So, tell me about your opponent," she said.

He wasn't sure if she was interested, or if she merely wanted to make small talk. In either case Jonas was happy to oblige. He needed to concentrate on his candidacy rather than the sexy woman seated beside him.

"His name is Roderick Davenport. He's a developer, in his late fifties. And he's currently on the board."

"He's not the incumbent?"

"No. The current Mayor decided not to run for re-election. It's an open seat and, thanks to the primary, it's come down to the two of us."

Serena nodded. "I assume, given his age, that Roderick Davenport is married?" She gave the name a fancy flourish.

"Going on thirty years."

"The man deserves a medal," she drawled. "What's your impression of him?"

"He's nice enough, in a superficial way. He says all the right things. He's never outwardly rude. But he has an edge." Jonas laughed wryly. "I get the feeling that deep down he would sell his mother if the price were right."

Serena laughed as well. "Wouldn't we all?"

Having met her mother, he wasn't sure she was joking…or that he blamed her.

The Citizens for Change dinner was in a ballroom at one of the city's largest resorts. The wait staff were still adding the finishing touches to the tables when Jonas and Serena arrived. Jameson, of course, was already there, pacing as he talked into the cellphone clipped to his ear. He ended the call when he spied them and hurried over.

"Jonas—about time."

"About time? We're early."

"I expected you ten minutes ago. Cocktail hour starts in less than thirty minutes." He turned then. "So, this is Serena?"

Jameson was clearly surprised, and the set of his mouth said not in a good way.

Serena had figured that out, too. She batted her eyelashes and drawled, "That's me. No doubt you're both wishing I was the one who got away."

"No jokes like that around the media, or anyone else for that matter," he chastised. "In fact don't speak at all unless spoken to first."

"Should I pretend to be mute?"

Jameson's face reddened, a sure sign that his blood pressure was rising. "Haven't you explained *anything* to her?" he demanded in exasperation.

"She'll be fine. Lighten up," Jonas replied, earning a curious glance from Serena.

Jameson didn't appear convinced. He tugged at his graying goatee. "Who selected this outfit?"

"I did. And I managed to do so all by myself."

"Of course you did." Jameson directed the rest of his reply to Jonas. "It will have to do for tonight, but I'll hire a stylist first thing in the morning. Serena will need something less…eye-catching for next week's debate. We want the media focus to be on you and your policies. Indeed, the less they focus on your new wife the better."

Serena opened her mouth to object, but Jameson steamrolled over whatever she'd been about to say.

"We'll make the announcement right after dinner. When you take the stage to give your speech, bring it up first thing. That way any reporters here covering the event will have to wait till the very end to ask questions. I've planted a few people in the audience to ask policy-related questions. I'll point them out when we're all seated. You're to call on them first.

"As for you, Serena, your homework for tonight is to watch the Davenports. In particular, pay close attention to Cindy. She's her husband's right hand, and a regular pro when it comes to mixing and mingling. You can learn a lot from her."

"Serena will do fine," Jonas said again. "She's a natural when it comes to putting people at ease and getting them to open up."

Serena cast a sideways glance at Jonas. This was the second time he'd made such a remark. His faith in her ability seemed genuine and helped chase away some of her nerves.

The butterflies were back in full force, however, when Jameson replied, "Cindy Davenport is better known in this community than her husband. Need I remind you that she sits on the boards of half a dozen non-profits? She has a lot of influential friends in this town."

"I'm not running against Cindy."

Jameson snorted. "Don't play dumb, Jonas. Spouses count for something in an election such as this. They can be an asset." The older man's gaze cut to Serena. "Or they can be a liability."

She bristled at the comment, since Jameson's tone left no doubt as to which category he felt she belonged in.

"Perhaps you could hire someone to take my place? Sort of like a stunt wife."

"I believe that's in effect what you are." The campaign manager's smile was benign, but the dig was sharp enough to draw blood.

"You're out of line," Jonas warned.

"I apologize, then." Jameson inclined his balding head. Even had his tone been sincere he would have ruined it with his next words. "I'm not expecting Serena to hold her own against a powerhouse partner like Cindy. My only goal for tonight is that she keeps from embarrassing either herself or you."

The cellphone clipped to his ear trilled. "I've got to take this." Before turning away, Jameson said, "Explain tonight's format to her, if you haven't done so already."

"It's going to be tough not to let all of his flattery go to my head," Serena muttered dryly when they were alone.

"Sorry. Jameson is a little intense."

"A couple more colorful descriptive phrases come to mind, but yours applies, too."

"Winning elections is his job."

"And your job depends on how well he does his?"

Jonas nodded. "But I won't allow him to talk to you that way. I meant it when I told him he was out of line."

Warmth bloomed inside her. "Thanks."

"Want a drink?"

"I don't know." She tipped her head to one side. "Is it on your campaign manager's list of approved activities for me?"

Half of Jonas's mouth crooked up. "Probably not."

"Then, yes, by all means. And make it a double."

He laughed. "You're not planning to get loaded and dance on the tabletops, are you?"

"Only if I can convince Saint Cindy to do the cha-cha with me."

"Knowing you, you probably could." His grin turned the words into a compliment. "To be on the safe side, we'd better make that double a glass of Chardonnay."

"Yes, we wouldn't want poor Jameson to suffer a massive stroke."

By the time they got their drinks from one of the bars that had been set up around the ballroom's perimeter Jameson was off the telephone and their reprieve was over. The older man honed in on them like a charging elephant. Even before he came to a complete stop he began issuing directives.

"Okay, we've got about fifteen minutes before the guests start to arrive. Here's how we're going to spin this. When people, especially anyone from the media, ask how the two of you met, you are to be vague."

"How vague?" Serena asked.

"You are to say that you were introduced through mutual friends, but don't offer any names." He tugged at his goatee. "I think it would look better if you left everyone with the impression that you met one another several years ago and recently reconnected."

"Got it," she replied, mimicking his über-intense expression. She thought she saw Jonas's lips twitch.

Jameson grabbed her hand and Jonas's arm and leaned in close. In a tone that bordered on snarling, he told them, "Under no circumstance are either of you to tell *anyone* that you've only known each other for a week—or, God help us all, that you exchanged vows mere hours after first meeting. If we get lucky, the tacky wedding chapel will get left out of the mix completely."

Tacky wedding chapel? Okay, maybe it had been a little on the kitschy side, but Jameson made everything about that night seem seedy, wrong. That wasn't how Serena remembered it.

Apparently Jonas had a different recollection, too. "The place wasn't as bad as all that."

"I agree. The Elvis impersonator who conducted our ceremony wasn't the sequined-jumpsuit-wearing sort. He channeled the younger Elvis—you know, the one who made all the girls swoon in the movies." There had been no such impersonator, but she wasn't able to resist.

Jameson made a strangled sound that had Serena trying to recall what she knew about resuscitation. She couldn't be sure from Jonas's expression, but she thought he might be holding back laughter.

"She's kidding," her husband said as he discreetly pulled his arm free of Jameson's death grip.

"This isn't a laughing matter." Jameson released her hand, but only so he could tug on his goatee again.

"I won't bring up Elvis or the chapel," Serena promised. "I'll stick to the script. Mutual friends introduced Jonas and me. We first met ages ago. When we saw each other something just…"

"Clicked?" Jonas supplied.

"Just clicked *again*," Jameson reminded them on a sigh. "You know, now that I think of it, how you originally met is bound to garner a lot of attention. People like to know the details when it comes to romantic tripe like that."

"You're single, aren't you?" Serena guessed.

"Since my divorce five years ago. And I plan to remain that way till I die, sweetheart."

That explained a lot. To think Serena considered *herself* jaded when it came to matters of the heart.

Jameson divided his gaze between her and Jonas as he suggested, "How about if we say that you met during a college break?"

"Sure." Jonas shrugged.

Serena shook her head. "I didn't go to college."

"She didn't go to college," Jameson muttered to no one in particular. Instead of tugging on his goatee, this time he massaged his temple.

"Serena is a gifted artist, Jameson. She hasn't needed a degree to land a job in her field. She's going places."

She blinked in surprise. Jonas's earnestness had her blinking—until she reminded herself that his assessment of her abilities might just be a clever soundbite uttered for his campaign manager's benefit.

Jameson's expression brightened fractionally. "Has your work been shown anywhere that we can plug?"

"Not exactly." She doubted the party in San Diego where her funky five-tiered, purple- and pink-iced confection honoring a girl's sweet sixteen had been unveiled today would count. "I decorate cakes for a living."

"Cakes." Jameson sighed. If the man kept rubbing his temple like that he was going to take off skin.

"They're really more like works of art," Jonas countered. "These aren't the kind the grocery store knocks out *en masse*. They are custom cakes that clients come in and specifically request."

"You've seen them?" Jameson asked. The question was on the tip of Serena's tongue as well.

"Yes. Earlier this week. I contacted the shop where she worked in La Jolla. Her boss—ex-boss now—isn't exactly the type to gush, but when I told her that Serena had some high-end, maybe even celebrity clients lined up here in Vegas—" he winked at Serena "—she emailed me several snapshots of incredible cakes and went on and on about her young protégé's abilities. Apparently she taught you everything you know."

Not exactly. But Heidi Bonaventure's overstatement wasn't why Serena had to struggle to keep her mouth from falling open. "You called her?"

"I did."

"And she…she…gushed?"

Jonas smiled. "She did. The word fawning comes to mind." He sobered a little. "You really are a gifted artist. I can say that even though I doubt those photographs did your work justice."

"You didn't have to contact her." Serena's throat constricted. She decided to look at the situation from a more practical side, since that made it easier to speak. "I mean, if you wanted to see samples you just had to ask. I have a photo album of my favorite cake designs. And, God, you didn't have to tell her I was being considered to make cakes for celebrities."

"I didn't *have* to tell her that," he agreed. "But since both a well-known singer and a high-profile actor may wind up calling her for a reference, I figured it was wise."

"Wh-what? You mean…?"

"It's not set in stone, which is why I haven't said anything. I have a friend who works at Caesar's Palace, where both these people are planning big parties."

She covered her mouth with one hand. There was a scream in there just waiting to burst free. When she was sure she could contain it, Serena removed the hand and said, "I'm walking on air, Jonas. This is incredible. Thank you."

"No problem. I said I'd help you out, remember?"

The bubble of happiness that had been growing burst unceremoniously. He was just trying to live up to his end of their bargain. Though it took an effort, she sidelined her disappointment.

"So you're already making good on your promises. That's a rarity for a politician, I believe. You get my vote." Serena managed a tight smile.

Jonas frowned. He looked confused, maybe even a little offended—which was ridiculous, Serena told herself. She'd only said it like it was.

Jameson was oblivious to their sudden tension. "When it's set in stone, tell me. We can use it. You know, it might even work in your favor that she's not college-educated. It makes you more approachable to the little guy."

"A true man of the people," Serena added dryly.

Jameson nodded vigorously even as she felt the urge to drop her chin to her chest and weep.

She raised it instead. Mustering as much dignity as she could, she said, "For the record, I *have* taken several evening classes at the community college, and a business course from USC online."

Jameson dismissed that in much the same way her father had. Jonas, however, smiled.

"My folks are friends with a professor at the Cordon Bleu College of Culinary Arts. It's a topnotch school, or so I've been told. He's retired now, and owns a restaurant just outside the city that's famous for its desserts. He's even made a few appearances on cable TV, judging various challenges."

"You're not talking about Jeffrey Kefron?"

He nodded, pleased. "I told him of your work and—"

"You told Jeffrey Kefron about my work?" she interrupted in disbelief.

"Yes. He said to send him photos and a copy of your résumé. If he likes what he sees, he might allow you into his kitchen for a few hours each week to shadow him or another pastry chef. You could learn some new techniques or perfect old ones."

Appearances, Serena reminded herself, when another silly bubble of happiness tried to rise to the surface.

"Great. Thanks. I appreciate it."

Jameson was more enthusiastic.

"I love it. Goes to show that it's never too late for self-improvement." His smile broadened. "And it mirrors the city's revitalization efforts and your support of them." He slapped Jonas on the back. "Good thinking,

Benjamin. But, then, this is exactly why you performed so well in the primary."

The room had started to fill. "Now, go mingle," Jameson instructed. "Start with the gentleman in the ill-fitting suit over there. He's a representative from the governor's office. It won't hurt to have an ally in the capital."

Her lack of a college education aside, Serena felt as if she'd just power-prepped for a midterm exam. Midterm? Make that a final, with ninety percent of her grade resting on how well she did. On how well she managed to hide her confusion and disappointment.

"Ready?" Jonas asked.

She pasted on a smile and threaded her arm through his, ignoring the zap of heat even such straightforward contact caused. They needed to look like a couple, a newly married, head-over-heels-in-love couple. He was holding up his end of the bargain. It was time for Serena to hold up hers.

"Let's do this."

Jonas marveled at Serena's stamina, as well as her sheer nerve. She was the center of attention, and not only because her vibrant green dress stood out amid a sea of bland hues. People were openly curious about the sexy young woman on Candidate Benjamin's arm. Other than his mother and older sister, he hadn't brought a member of the opposite sex to any of his campaign functions. But she never bowed her head or tried to duck a conversation. She kept her chin up. When she didn't understand the facts behind a business's zoning appeal she admitted as much, and then asked questions. Ditto when someone raised the subject of an attempt the previous fall to increase taxes. The proposal had failed at the polls, and now there was talk about cutting services, including police and fire protection.

"What do you think of that, Mr. Benjamin?" one of the guests asked bluntly. "Would you favor such a move?"

"Public safety always will be a priority of Jonas's administration," Serena said emphatically, before he could answer.

After the man left she sent Jonas a sheepish smile. "I guess I should have let you reply. But I'm right about that, aren't I?"

She looked relieved when he nodded. "You are."

Throughout the mingling, he introduced her as Serena Warren. Her decision to keep her maiden name worked to their advantage.

Per Jameson's instructions, he kept the introductions short and avoided any mention of their marriage. That would come later. After the last dessert cup was cleared from the tables he would take to the stage and make the big announcement, just prior to launching into his prepared remarks.

Dread pooled in his stomach as the hour approached. He didn't want to make the announcement. Not because of the commotion it was bound to cause and the questions it would raise. Not even because of the possible hit his campaign could take. The disturbing truth was he wanted to keep Serena and their relationship to himself for a while longer.

They were married, but they'd never dated. They'd made love, but neither of them was sure of their feelings. He was drawn to Serena, physically attracted beyond the point of sanity, but it was more than that. Given time, he might be able to figure out the exact reason for her allure. Time, unfortunately, wasn't a luxury he had.

Lost in thought, Jonas didn't notice Roderick and Cindy Davenport approaching until they were upon him.

"My worthy opponent," Roderick said with

a mocking bow. Then he offered a hand. "Good to see you."

"Same here." Jonas smiled at the man's wife. "Nice to see you, too, Mrs. Davenport."

"Cindy, please. Mrs. Davenport makes me feel old enough to be your mother."

She *was*, in fact, old enough to be his mother. Jonas merely smiled. "This is Serena."

"You're a lovely young thing," Roderick said, covering her hand with both of his. "I can see why Jonas has kept you to himself until tonight. I wouldn't want to share either."

"Stop, dear. You're embarrassing yourself, not to mention this poor girl," Cindy inserted in a bored tone. She ran a hand over the double strand of pearls at her neck and regarded Serena with a critical eye. "That dress is…very green."

Serena's chin rose fractionally. "Thank you. Green is Jonas's favorite color."

He smiled in agreement, though it wasn't…or hadn't been until tonight.

"Well, you certainly know how to stand out in a crowd." It was clear Cindy didn't mean it as a compliment. "All eyes are on you, my dear."

Exactly what Jameson had said he didn't want to happen. Yet Jonas couldn't muster any regret. He reached for Serena's hand. Her fingers were cold—possibly from the air-conditioning, more likely from nerves.

"Serena would stand out in a crowd even if she wore…boring taupe and granny pearls."

He'd merely intended to reference the assertion Serena had made earlier in the day. Too late he realized that Roderick's wife was outfitted in a staid suit of that very color, along with the aforementioned jewelry. Jonas would have swallowed hard if not for the foot in his mouth.

"I'm going to guess that Jameson wouldn't approve of you insulting your opponent's wife," Serena mused, after the Davenports excused themselves and stalked away.

"I wasn't trying to." He shrugged. "Cindy insulted you first."

"Yes, but she was a little more subtle about it." Serena smiled. "Well, at least dinner will be interesting."

An hour later both couples and their key campaign people sat around the table closest to the podium, making awkward small talk as they ate dinner and waited for the program to begin. The evening's format was simple. First Jonas and his opponent would have fifteen minutes each to sum up their main points.

Jonas would take the podium first, per the outcome of a coin-toss. After each man finished, the president of Citizens for Change would go through the audience with a cordless microphone to take questions. The candidates wouldn't have a chance to pick the questioners. So much for the people Jameson had planted in the audience to steer the conversation away from Jonas's marriage.

As it was, speculation was building to a fever pitch as to who Serena was, where she had come from, and the exact nature of her relationship with Jonas. Roderick Davenport's campaign manager, Lyle Perry, was especially curious, plying her with questions about her background and political leanings, all under the guise of small talk. She handled herself well, answering truthfully but without imparting too much information. Nothing she said could be twisted around. Even Jameson looked pleased with her performance.

"She's doing well, isn't she?" Jonas whispered to the older man as servers cleared the dishes from their table.

"She hasn't committed a major *faux pas*," was Jameson's grudging reply.

"People love her. Admit it. You were wrong to be so concerned."

"She's still a liability, Jonas. If Davenport gets wind of the fact that you married her on a whim, he'll paint you as an impulsive fool unfit for high office and a lot of voters will agree with him. Make no mistake. That woman is your Achilles' heel."

Serena kicked off her stilettos the moment they were seated in Jonas's car. Talk about a baptism by fire. She was glad the night was over. Not only did her arches ache, her cheeks were sore from smiling and her voice had grown hoarse from all the talking she'd done in the two hours since their marriage had become a matter of public record. But that wasn't the reason she was so quiet on the drive to the condo. As Jameson had feared, their surprise nuptials had dominated the question-and-answer period. Jonas had kept his answers brief and simple and held to the script. He and Serena had met several years earlier and dated briefly before going their separate ways. They'd reconnected when she came to Vegas with her girl-friends. They'd married. Yada-yada-yada. Blah-blah-blah.

Outright lies and half-truths. Serena didn't like it.

She could only imagine what the reporters who'd been on hand would write. As they'd waited for the valet to bring around the car, Jameson had warned them to expect a variety of media outlets to call in the days ahead, seeking interviews and asking for specifics.

Would they be able to keep everything straight?

"You're quiet," Jonas said.

"Just tired," she murmured, even as her mind whirled.

He glanced over. "You seem more introspective than exhausted."

He knew her too well. Tonight that thought was far from comforting. She felt raw and exposed as it was, even though the real Serena had hardly been on display, green dress notwithstanding.

"I feel like I'm back in grade school learning lines for a play," she mused as he slowed for a red light. "I was never good at learning lines. I always screwed them up, saying the wrong thing at the wrong time. I'm better at ad libbing."

I'm better at being myself, she added silently.

"You did fine. Better than fine. You were magnificent."

"Luck."

Jonas sent her a wink just before the light turned green. "In this town, luck counts for a lot."

CHAPTER NINE

FOR the next several days Serena kept a low profile, venturing outside the condo on a couple of occasions and then only with Jonas by her side. Jameson thought it best that she did not interact with the press on her own just yet.

As it was, reporters were calling the condo at all hours of the day and night seeking comment. The story of her and Jonas's hasty marriage had grown legs—especially since one of the more enterprising in their ranks had discovered the nuptials had taken place in one of the city's ubiquitous chapels. Jameson had done his best to spin the facts, saying it had been done as a good-natured nod to one of the city's more flamboyant industries, and a more traditional ceremony and reception were in the works for later.

Another lie added to the many they already had to keep straight.

* * *

Jonas turned the key in the lock late on Friday. It had been a long week and an especially long day, both at the office and afterward at his downtown campaign headquarters, where he'd rallied the troops for another weekend of door-to-door campaigning. Jonas was a firm believer in the old-fashioned technique. Voters wanted to feel that they could relate to a candidate, connect with him beyond the ballot box. In an age of emails and other impersonal means of communication, when the person running for public office, or a member of his campaign, showed up at the door to answer questions and drop off literature it was especially effective.

Jonas was glad to be home—eager to put his feet up and relax. Not that he managed to do much of that around Serena. It wasn't only because he found her sexy as hell. Though they were married and living together, they were essentially strangers.

He'd learned a little bit about her during the past week—trivial stuff like how she took her coffee and that she liked to read the back of the cereal box while she ate breakfast. He was eager to learn more. Spending a quiet night in seemed a good idea since he'd worked late the past two.

He'd picked up a couple of movies on his way home. One was a chick-flick based on a bestselling book of the same name. The woman at the rental place had suggested he keep a box of tissues on hand. Indeed, she'd gotten misty-eyed just thinking about the ending. The other was old-school horror—not a remake of a classic, but an original that had been digitally restored to all of its gory glory. He figured he knew which one she would pick. He'd watch the slasher flick later in his bedroom. God knew, he wouldn't be able to sleep. The past week had been torture, pure and simple. Knowing Serena was just across the hall had his libido humming on high.

After dropping off his briefcase in the foyer, he went to look for her. He found her in the kitchen, putting the finishing touches to dinner. She hadn't lied about not being a very good cook, but she'd given it her best shot all week. Salads were her forte—leafy greens tossed with sliced up hard-boiled eggs and bits of deli ham. For tonight's main dish, though, she'd used the oven. The dishtowel was tucked around her waist again. His fingers itched to remove it…as well as the rest of her clothing.

"Hey, Jonas."

"Smells good," he managed. His voice

cracked like an adolescent boy's on the second word.

She smiled. "Hope you like lasagna. I was tired of salads."

"I love it. Can I help with anything?"

"No, thanks. I'm almost done."

Despite her assurances, he set the movies he'd rented on the counter. "How about some wine?"

"Just half a glass for me. I'm meeting Alex for drinks a little later." Her gaze cut to the movies and she grimaced. Her tone half-hearted, she offered, "I can cancel."

"No. That's all right."

"Maybe we can watch them tomorrow night."

"It's not a big deal." Or it shouldn't have been. But he was disappointed.

Serena sighed. "I have to get out of here, Jonas. I've been in this condo for the better part of a week. I've had a lot to do, and, truthfully, I wasn't too eager to meet up with reporters and photographers on my own. But running errands with you isn't cutting it. I'm getting stir crazy."

He felt like a heel. He should have realized that, given her outgoing nature, Serena would get bored. Selfishly, though, he'd enjoyed having her almost exclusively to himself in the evenings, even if they always went their separate ways not long after the dinner dishes were cleared. She closeted herself in her bedroom with her laptop. Sometimes he heard her talking on the telephone. Neither method of social interaction, however, could take the place of seeing a friend face-to-face, sharing a laugh and a drink.

"You should have said something. You're not a prisoner here."

"I know. I'll try my best to dodge the media."

"'No comment' works in a pinch."

She smiled. "I won't be out too late. I might even be back in time to watch the shamelessly gratuitous bloodbath that takes place at the end of *Nightmare on Halloween*." She grinned. "That's assuming you watch the tearjerker first."

"I rented that one for you. I was only going to suffer through it if you wanted to watch it."

"Gee, thanks. For the record, I don't like movies with tragic endings." She grinned again. "Well, unless someone is holding a chainsaw and vowing enough revenge to warrant a sequel."

Another bit of trivia. He smiled.

They finished eating half an hour later.

When Serena pushed back her chair and reached for her plate he waved her hands away. "I'll take care of the table. You go get ready for your evening out."

"Are you sure you're okay with this?"

She was asking about more than the dishes. Jonas nodded. "It's only fair. You cooked. I should clean up."

The kitchen was soon put back to rights and the dishwasher was finishing its first cycle. Jonas had changed into a pair of comfortable jeans and a worn tee-shirt that sported the name of his alma mater, and was seated on the couch, going over the results of a likely voter poll that his campaign had commissioned, when Serena came down the hall from the guestroom. The four percentage points by which he was leading were forgotten.

Serena wore a cap-sleeved blouse that was a couple of shades darker than her hair, and a short skirt whose funky black and white geometric print was the only thing that kept Jonas from ogling her legs. He dragged his gaze back to her face with an effort.

She was gaping, too.

"Something wrong?" he asked.

"You're wearing jeans."

"I do own a few pairs," he said, more amused than insulted.

"I've never seen you in them. Or a shirt that didn't button up." She appeared to sigh. "You look good."

He'd never received a compliment for dressing down before. He wasn't sure how to react—especially given the way Serena was eyeing him. His body had no such problem. Jonas decided to change the subject.

"So, where are you and Alex going?"

"Hennessey's Tavern. Ever been?"

"A few times." The Irish pub wasn't far from the condo, and impossible to miss given the huge lighted glass of ale that hung over the entrance. "They make a good black and tan, if that's your thing." When she wrinkled her nose, he said, "Their Bloody Marys are pretty good, too. You and your friend will enjoy yourselves."

"I know we will. I'm eager to see her and catch up. The venue doesn't really matter."

"Are you homesick, Serena?"

"Homesick?" She pursed her lips. "I wouldn't say that. As you probably gathered after meeting Buck and Susanne, I'm not exactly tight with my folks. My friends?" Her shoulders rose. "I miss them. In San Diego we did a lot together, so it's a real break for me that Alex is in Vegas working. I'm in pretty regular contact with Jayne and Molly, too." She smiled. "The wonders of technology. It helps to make the world very small."

"But texting, emails and phone calls aren't the same."

The corners of her mouth tugged down. "No. But I'll be back in San Diego eventually."

He'd already told Serena her friends were welcome to come, but he wanted to give her something to help make her stay in Vegas easier. Jonas glanced around his living room. It was nice enough, tasteful and tidy. Okay, maybe a little boring. Before Serena, he'd never questioned the décor or furniture placement. He did now.

"You know, if you'd like to redecorate the condo, you could."

"You'd let me do that?"

"Why not? Maybe that would make it feel more like home to you."

But it wasn't her home. That much came through loud and clear when she smiled politely and shook her head.

"Nah. I won't be here for very long." Serena pulled the strap of her hobo bag securely onto her shoulder. "I'd better be going."

He didn't want her to leave. But whether

that was just for tonight or at some point in the future, he couldn't be sure.

"I'll drive you." He set aside the paperwork and started to rise. He'd planned to lease a car for her use, but so far they hadn't had a chance to look for one.

"That's all right. It's not far, and I need the exercise. Have a good night, Jonas."

He lowered himself back onto the couch. "You too."

After the condo's door closed behind Serena it took all of Jonas's willpower not to go after her.

"Everything okay?" Alex asked as they sipped Bloody Marys. They'd started out in a booth inside Hennessey's, but when the music began they'd asked for an outdoor table so they could have a conversation without shouting. The people-watching was prime outdoors, too. Whether tourist or local, some very interesting folks marched past on Fremont.

"Fine. I just have a lot on my mind."

"Jonas?"

"I need to keep fact from fantasy." Serena lifted the stalk of celery out of the tomato-juice-based drink and bit off the end.

"Are you having difficulty distinguishing one from the other where he's concerned?"

Serena told her friend about a trip to the grocery store earlier in the week, during which they'd been snapped by a news photographer. The picture of her and Jonas picking out produce had made the front page of the *Sun*.

"I saw it. You looked cute."

"But it's all a lie," Serena argued.

The photo's caption had read: *"Mayoral candidate Jonas Benjamin beams at his new bride, Serena Warren, as she selects zucchini at Duke's Food World."*

In the photo, while her attention was focused on the menial task at hand, Jonas was smiling at her, his expression just this side of intimate.

"Are you sure about that? It looked pretty authentic to me," Alex said softly. "You guys looked like a real couple."

"It was a trick of the camera. Or more likely a trick of the campaign." Harsh laughter scraped her throat as she recalled what the rest of the caption had said: *"Could this be Las Vegas's next first couple?"* "Don't believe everything you see or read in the newspaper. When it comes to me and Jonas, nothing is what it seems."

"Are you sure?" Alex asked again. "Maybe that's just a convenient excuse you're hiding behind so you don't have to risk your heart."

It wasn't what Serena wanted to hear, given her tangled emotions. She didn't want them to be the result of anything other than lust. Nor did she want her marriage to be the result of anything other than good spontaneity gone bad. Otherwise it meant she was vulnerable.

She didn't want to be vulnerable.

"You know my feelings on long-term relationships, Alex. They don't work out. Look at my parents. Thirty years of wedded misery."

"That's their choice."

"Okay, look at Jayne. God, Rich claimed to love her, and then he all but destroyed her with his lies. In the meantime, *I* thought he was a pretty good guy."

"He had us all fooled. Jayne will rise from the ashes and be all the better for it."

"And what about Molly's ex? Huh? Dr. Doug?" Serena sneered. "From what little she's said on the subject of their divorce it's clear they wanted different things from their marriage, which is why Molly is flying solo these days."

"Every relationship doesn't work out," Alex agreed. For a moment her expression turned wistful. "Doesn't mean someone can't surprise you, you know?"

"Are we talking about Jonas?"

Alex straightened in her seat. "Of course. Who else would we be talking about?"

"Your boss, perhaps? You can't fool me. Molly and Jayne let it slip that you and Wyatt kissed recently." Serena grinned, happy to let her friend take a turn in the hot seat.

But Alex was too smart for that. "We aren't here to talk about me and my boss. I promised the girls I'd be here to support you, Mrs. Benjamin! But maybe you shouldn't write off things with Jonas before you figure out if you want something more from each other than s—" She coughed.

"Sex? Go ahead—you can say it." Sex was all Serena had thought about since she and Jonas had started sharing a household and not having any. "He wears really great cologne," she murmured absently.

Alex sipped her drink and said nothing, although her raised eyebrows invited Serena to go on.

"It's sinful. After he left for work the other morning I actually slipped into his bathroom, uncapped the bottle, and then stood there for a good fifteen minutes inhaling deeply." She swore she could smell it now.

"That's—"

"Pathetic. I know." She took another bite of celery.

Alex shook her head. "Actually, I was going to say telling."

"Nothing telling about it. It's just a physical reaction. To his scent, to his gorgeous face, to his killer body." Although Serena also liked his sense of humor, his intellect, his thoughtfulness. Which had her recalling something. "Tonight he told me I could redecorate his condo if I wanted."

"Really?" Alex blinked.

"It has this half-hearted Tuscan vibe going. It's not really my taste. I don't think it's his, either. I'm figuring he gave an interior decorator free rein."

"And now he's offering you the same? Interesting. Are you going to?"

Serena started to shake her head. She'd already told Jonas no. But… "Maybe."

"Maybe, hmm?"

She finished off the stalk of celery and changed the subject. She didn't like the way Alex was watching her.

* * *

It wasn't quite midnight when Serena arrived home. She and Alex had parted with the promise to meet up again soon. Jonas was still in the living room, seated on the sofa. His head was back. His feet were bare and propped on the ottoman. He was sound asleep, despite the blood-curdling screams coming from the television.

She crossed the room, removed the DVD and switched off both the player and the television. Jonas didn't stir. In the silence that followed Serena stepped closer and studied him. A day's worth of beard growth shaded his jaw—and, boy, he looked good in those jeans. So approachable. So relaxed. So much more like the man she'd married—even if he'd been outfitted by Armani then.

She wanted to sit down on the couch next to him and curl into his side. She backed toward the hall instead, and bumped into a potted ficus tree, nearly sending it toppling. Jonas stirred. His eyes opened. A sexy smile tilted up the corners of his lips when he spied her. It, too, was warm and welcoming.

"Hey." He rubbed the sleep from his eyes. "You're home."

At that moment, before Serena could rationalize the feeling away, that was exactly how she felt. It was also exactly why, after a brisk nod, she bolted to her bedroom.

CHAPTER TEN

ANOTHER couple of weeks passed. More of Serena's belongings arrived via parcel post and were unpacked and put away. Though she hadn't accepted Jonas's offer to redecorate the condo, she'd decided a little tweaking of her own room's décor was in order. She'd swapped the colorless comforter for her violet duvet, and a zebra-print area rug broke up the beige of the carpet. The top of the dresser sported an assortment of framed photographs—most of them of herself with Jayne, Alex and Molly. Thank God for telephones, texting and email. Even though they were all busy, they managed to connect daily.

Only one photo on the dresser—the smallest of them all since it was an old Polaroid—was of her family. In the picture Serena was five and sitting atop her father's shoulders. She remembered the day clearly.

They'd been living in Norfolk, Virginia, then. Her father had been stationed at the naval base and his ship, the *USS Shreveport*, had just returned to port after six months in the Mediterranean Sea. Buck was in his dress whites. His face was tanned and he was actually smiling as he held on to his daughter's legs. Serena remembered him saying that the world was changing, that women were making inroads in the military. Maybe she'd make a good sailor someday. Of course she'd known, even then, that a naval career wasn't what she wanted. But she'd enjoyed the positive attention from her hard-to-please father.

Serena's mother stood next to them. Susanne's hand was resting on Buck's upper arm. Serena recalled that they'd kissed on the lips upon his return. The image had stayed with her to this day, since she'd rarely witnessed any intimacy between them. Susanne's expression had been as close to happy as Serena could recall ever seeing it. They'd all been happy that day. Peace had reigned until well into the evening. Perhaps that was why she'd framed the photograph and kept it all these years. She'd needed one piece of evidence that, if only briefly, her parents had shared a bond that went beyond duty—that they had, if only for a day, been the kind of family that existed in greeting card commercials.

She studied the photo now as she tidied up her room. Jonas had called earlier. Since Serena's arrival in Vegas they'd managed to avoid his mother and sister, but the reprieve was over. His father was in town and they had been summoned to the family estate for dinner. Serena was dreading it. Her own parents had a hard time accepting her for who she was. She could only imagine how the conservative Benjamin clan would react, their knowledge of the sham marriage notwithstanding.

What did one wear to meet a man's parents?

Serena had never had to answer that question before. She'd never dated a man long enough to have to figure it out. Even though they would be dining in at Jonas's folks' estate, half an hour outside the city, she had little doubt something more formal than cropped jeans and a midriff-baring tee-shirt would be expected, so she called Alex.

"What are you *thinking* of wearing?" her friend asked.

"I'm too busy having a panic attack to think. Jonas's father is a Congressman, Alex.

He and Mrs. Benjamin belong to a country club," Serena all but wailed.

"They're just people."

Serena ignored the comment. "Tell me what you would wear."

"It doesn't matter what I would wear, because I'm not the one going. Be yourself, Serena." Alex's tone was gentle but firm.

"Right. Be myself." She flopped back on the bed. "Like *that* would go over big."

"It's what snagged Jonas's attention in the first place."

"This isn't about a guy in a bar."

"Neither was that. Even though I wasn't there, I don't think you're being fair to him or you. But that's not my point," she continued before Serena could interject. "No news cameras will be at the Benjamins' estate, and you told me Jonas's parents know why the two of you haven't annulled your marriage yet. Be yourself. What do you have to lose?"

"Nothing." And everything.

Despite her long-held aversion to commitment, Serena had feelings for her husband. As terrifying as she found the prospect, she thought she might be in love with him. That would explain a lot. And it could mean that her wild roll of the dice had been a calculated move after all. Yes, that was how *she* was beginning to feel, but what about Jonas?

The doorbell rang just as Serena hung up. A woman stood in the hall. She was model-tall, not to mention model-slim, and perfectly proportioned everywhere else. Her honey-blonde hair hung just past her shoulders. A white headband held it back from her face; her crystalline blue eyes regarded Serena shrewdly.

The woman's smile was saccharin-sweet. "You must be Serena."

"I am. Can I help you?"

"I'm Janet. Janet Kincaid." The woman said it expectantly, as if Serena should know who she was.

Reporter, she figured. Television, given her looks. My, they were relentless. The doorman had been good about keeping members of the media from sneaking upstairs. Apparently he'd given this one a pass because of her pretty face and long legs.

"Thank you for stopping by, Janet. But my husband is at his office right now, and I'm in the middle of something. You'll have to talk to Jameson Culver if you want to set up an interview with either of us. Our schedules are pretty full these days."

"I'm not here for an interview." Janet's

laughter echoed in the hallway. *Silly girl*, it seemed to say. "I've been vacationing at my parents' villa in the Italian countryside the past couple of months. I only recently returned to the States and learned of Jonas's marriage. I was coming by to congratulate him. Oh, and you too, of course."

"Of course." Nothing like being tacked on as an afterthought. Even as she seethed, Serena smiled blandly at Janet. "I'll be sure to tell Jonas that you were here."

"I'm sure you will. Maybe we can meet for a celebratory round of drinks?"

"That sounds wonderful. We'll be in touch our first free evening." *After hell freezes over.*

"Terrific. Let me know, and I'll make reservations at our favorite place." Janet pretended to act flustered then. "Oh, well, maybe another spot would be more appropriate."

Serena knew she was going to regret asking, but even though she suspected, she suddenly had to know. "How is it exactly that you and Jonas know one another?"

"Oh, my…" Blondie pressed a manicured hand to her perfectly proportioned chest. "I thought you knew. Jonas and I used to date."

"You dated?" Serena didn't want to

believe it, but the evidence was there. Janet was so his type.

"Yes, for five years."

The number landed like a grenade. Five years? That wasn't dating. That was practically a lifetime together—at least in dog years.

Janet glanced past Serena into the condo. "The place hasn't changed much since I was here last, although the television over the fireplace is new." She chuckled delicately. "Men and their flatscreens. They certainly like them large."

"Don't they, though?"

"I see that he kept the color scheme." Her smile bordered on smug. "I picked it out."

Ah, so the watered-down Tuscan décor was *Janet's* doing. She'd marked the place much as a dog marked its territory. Now Serena's hackles rose.

"Actually, we're in the process of changing it." She wrinkled her nose. "It's not really my taste. Nor is it Jonas's."

It wasn't exactly a lie. Hadn't he told Serena she could make over the room? Didn't that imply he'd grown tired of it?

The other woman's eyes narrowed. "He loved it."

Serena let her shrug serve as a reply.

"Well, I won't keep you," Janet said. "You mentioned you're busy."

Serena embellished the truth. "Yes. I have some last-minute errands to run before Jonas and I have dinner with his family tonight."

"I'd heard the Congressman was in town. Lovely people, the Benjamins. Please give them my regards." Janet started to leave, but turned back. "I hope you'll forgive me for saying so, but I'm surprised Jonas has married."

"Married me, or got married at all?"

"Both. Sorry." But Janet's smile was shrewd rather than apologetic. "I gave him an ultimatum, you know."

"After five years of dating I can understand why."

Janet's smile grew brittle. "Yes. Well, he said he wasn't ready to make a lifetime commitment—that relationships require careful layering, and that's the only way to build a proper and lasting foundation."

Didn't that sound just like Jonas? But Serena shrugged. "I guess he changed his mind."

"I saw his mother just the other day. Actually, I stopped by to see her. Our families have known one another for years. They belong to the same country club." Of course they did. "She hinted that the two of you had just—well, jumped into marriage blindly."

My specialty, Serena thought. "Your point?"

"No point, really. I just want to let you know—to let *both* of you know—that I'll be here for Jonas when things don't work out."

"Don't you mean *if*?"

"No. Mrs. Benjamin hinted that neither of you was without regrets." Now Janet's smile was more like a baring of teeth. The gloves were off. No more niceties. Her gaze dissected Serena's appearance. Afterward, she shook her head. "I only hope, for his sake, that you don't cost him the Mayor's race in the meantime."

After Janet left, Serena was furious. She took it out on the tepid Tuscan décor, backhanding an olive throw pillow before jabbing a red one with her fist. The fight went out of her quickly, though, mostly because she knew it was born of jealousy.

This time, instead of striking a pillow, Serena slumped onto the couch and hugged one to her aching heart. She knew exactly what her husband saw—what any man in his position would see—in someone like Janet. The woman was perfect. Political Wife

Barbie brought to scale and come to life. As for why he hadn't married Janet, that was obvious. No man liked to be given an ultimatum. Serena tortured herself now by wondering if he regretted not accepting it.

She was still seated on the couch, awash in self-doubt, when he arrived home an hour later.

"You haven't forgotten about dinner with my parents?" he asked.

"No. I...the time got away. Sorry." She rose to her feet and started for the hall before she realized she was still holding the pillow to her chest. Tossing it back on to the couch she said, "Oh, by the way, I've decided to take you up on your offer to redecorate this room."

Jonas blinked in surprise. "You have?"

"Problem?" she asked defiantly.

"No. No problem. I just... Why the sudden change of heart?"

No way was Serena going to mention his ex-girlfriend's visit, or Janet's offer to *be there* for Jonas once Serena was out of the picture.

So she shrugged. "You know me. I like to be spontaneous."

In her bedroom, Serena nibbled her lip. Now more than ever she was at a loss for what to wear. After meeting Janet and seeing how the woman dressed there was no way she was going to pass muster with the Benjamins. On an oath, she shook off her self-pity. She wouldn't try.

Be yourself, Alex had suggested.

That was exactly who Serena was going to be.

She fished through her closet and came out with a loud paisley print sundress that she paired with a tangle of cheap beaded necklaces and bright red heels. She pulled her hair back in a French braid and donned her favorite earrings—the chandeliers she'd worn the night she and Jonas met. Eyeing her reflection in the full-length mirror that graced the back of the closet door, she smiled. She wasn't the wife of the candidate tonight. She'd never be mistaken for a member of the country club set. Oddly, that gave her confidence.

She would indeed be herself, and to hell with what the Benjamins, including Jonas, thought.

Jonas was nervous as he prepared for the evening. He wasn't worried about what his parents and sister would say or do when they met his bride. They would be polite and gracious. They were always polite and gracious to company, and despite Serena's status as his wife they would consider her as such. They knew, after all, that the marriage was destined for annulment.

He frowned as he tucked his shirt into the herringbone trousers he'd just gotten back from the cleaners. No, he wasn't worried about his folks' reaction. He was worried about what Serena would think of them and, by extension, of him.

He studied his reflection. The tailored shirt and the tie his personal shopper had picked out to go with the herringbone suit matched perfectly. He closed his eyes and sighed. God, did Serena find him as boring as he looked?

He already knew that she found his appearance stuffy at times, and that she thought he was way too conservative—not just in the way he dressed but in how he approached life. Yes, he liked order, and his career demanded a wardrobe that consisted mainly of tailored suits, but he hadn't considered himself rigid or humorless until he'd viewed himself through her eyes.

Truth be told, when Jonas was around Serena qualities he hadn't known he possessed came to the fore. It turned out he could be outrageous—kissing a woman he didn't know in public—and spontaneous. Their marriage later that same night was proof of that.

He rubbed his chin. Or maybe it was proof of something else. Maybe it was proof that the man who seemed to live his life by a proscribed set of rules had been waiting for someone to show him how to color outside the lines.

His mood brightened. Next week he would ask Serena to accompany him shopping—maybe help him pick out some casual clothes beyond khakis. For tonight, the suit would have to do.

When Serena joined him in the living room half an hour later he struggled to catch his breath. Her sundress was bold, her jewelry a chaotic mess. Her only bow to formality had been to secure her wild red hair. Even so, a few rebel strands had unfurled around her face. No other woman of his acquaintance would attempt such a look, much less pull it off with such panache. Serena was absolutely lovely.

She didn't fit in with his family. He knew that even before they arrived at his parents' home and joined them, Elizabeth and her work-obsessed husband Oliver in the formal dining room. It wasn't only her clothing, but her animation and easy laughter. She was a peacock in a room full of mourning doves. Jonas had anticipated that she would make an impression. He hadn't figured his mother and sister would find her so interesting and amusing. Their laughter and conversation were genuine, and hardly the result of good manners.

"No wonder she didn't like the ring I selected," Elizabeth mused half under her breath as dessert was served. "You might have mentioned how extroverted she is."

"The word Jameson uses is *flashy*."

"Jameson would find Mother Teresa flashy."

"True," he agreed.

"She's holding her own with Dad. That's no small feat."

Elizabeth was right, but Jonas knew from experience that his father's expectations ran exceptionally high.

A little later, when they retired to the veranda for drinks, his mother whispered, "She's very different from Janet—and I mean that as a compliment."

"So you like Serena?"

"She's refreshingly open and approachable. Besides, I see the way you look at her. How can I not like her?" She patted his cheek. "Maybe the mistake you told us you made is really a blessing in disguise."

His mother and sister's support made it a

little easier to face his father later when the men—minus Elizabeth's husband, who'd had to take a phone call—were alone in the study, enjoying aged cognac while the women took a walk in the lighted gardens.

Corbin started in right away. "I can see what the attraction was. The girl is beautiful. But if you had to go and do something stupid, couldn't you have done it with someone who could help your political career?"

"Amazingly, Dad, politics isn't at the center of my thought-process twenty-four-seven."

His father ignored the barb and went on. "In a town like Vegas a flamboyant wife might win you some points. But it's a good thing she'll be out of the picture before you turn your attention to Carson City or Washington."

Out of the picture. The words struck like daggers. He wasn't ready to argue with them. He turned to a safer difference of opinion. "How many times do I have to tell you I'm not interested in the governorship, or following you to D.C.?"

Corbin was shaking his head even before Jonas finished. "Of course you are. Once you get a taste of it—"

"No!" Jonas's reply echoed in the room as he shot to his feet. "I'm not you, Dad. Our dreams, our goals—they're different. I think I can do some good in Las Vegas, which is why I decided to become a candidate. But it doesn't mean I want to spend the rest of my life raising funds and running for this office or that. If I win, when my term as Mayor expires I might seek a second one. But that will be it. Afterward I'll return to my law practice. Am I making myself clear?"

"This young woman has really turned your head."

Per usual, his father had missed the point entirely. "My decision has nothing to do with Serena. I've felt this way for years."

"I know you've expressed reservations in the past—"

"Quit trying to spin my words. I haven't expressed reservations. I've out and out said it's not what I want."

Corbin sipped his drink. "You could have such a bright future in politics."

"It's not a future I want. When are you going to accept that?"

Jonas thought he might be getting through, until Corbin asked, "Did you marry Serena to force me accept it? Did you think that by marrying someone so unsuitable you'd finally stop me from trying to change your mind?"

"One has nothing to do with the other, and Serena isn't unsuitable."

Corbin scoffed. "Please. You've never brought a woman remotely like her around before."

"She's different," Jonas agreed slowly. "That doesn't make her unsuitable."

"But what about Janet? She's well-educated, attractive, and knows how to conduct herself in public."

"We broke up months ago, Dad."

"I know. But everyone, myself included, thought the two of you would get back together. You have so much in common."

"It only seemed that way."

Which was why it had taken Jonas so long to figure out what a bad match they made. Which was why he'd hidden behind the rationale of building layers when in reality all he'd been doing was postponing the inevitable. He'd liked and respected Janet, but the idea of spending the rest of his life with her had made him feel as if he were suffocating. Not so with Serena. He'd never felt more sure of anything than he had when he'd asked her to marry him. It had only been afterward that Jonas had let the doubts creep in.

The older man's eyes narrowed. "But you

don't plan to stay with Serena. At some point after the election your marriage will be quietly annulled and you'll go your separate ways."

Yes, that had been the plan. Jonas swirled the last of the cognac around in his glass and said nothing as a new plan began to take hold.

The weeks that followed passed faster than Serena had expected them to. Life with Jonas fell into a predictable yet hardly boring routine. The evenings often found them out, meeting with voters and eating mass-produced meals. When they were home Serena cooked dinner, broadening her repertoire from salads and pasta to baked chicken and even a marinated flank steak that had turned out edible despite being a little overdone.

Their days were full, too. Jonas spent his at his law office downtown. Serena spent hers putting together plans for her cake boutique and perfecting her craft. Unfortunately the Caesar's Palace gig had fallen through. Still, she was grateful to Jonas for even attempting to get her foot in the door. In the meantime Serena had contacted Jeffrey Kefron and forwarded her résumé and pictures of her cake designs. Fingers crossed, all that was left was to wait for his response.

To keep from thinking about it too much, she'd started on the living room remodeling. The design she had in mind leaned toward modern. She'd taken her cues from a magazine and from Jonas. The blue that was going up on the walls was in the same family as the robin-egg blue in his duvet cover, but a little more vibrant, leaning toward turquoise. The green she'd picked to go with it was to anchor the room. It would be used for the upholstery and window treatments. Yellow was the wow factor. As such it would be used sparingly. Just a few touches of it, scattered about the room.

She was standing on a ladder painting a wall when he arrived home one evening. Most of the furniture had been shoved to the center of the room, and she'd thrown an old blanket over the couch.

He set his keys and briefcase aside and glanced around. "You've been busy."

"Hope you don't mind. I got the urge to paint today." She climbed down from the ladder and set the roller back in the pan. Tucking her hands in the back pockets of her stained jeans, she asked, "What do you think of the color?"

"I like it. And that includes the speckles on

your nose." He brushed his fingers over them before motioning to the wall-mounted television. "Are you going to paint around the flatscreen?"

She laughed. "No. I left it for you to take down. I wasn't sure what to make of the wiring."

"I'll get it. Um, do I need to do it tonight?"

"Yes. I'm not planning to stop until I'm finished."

She didn't. It took the better part of the night, but it went much faster because Jonas changed into old clothes, grabbed a brush and gave her a hand.

Later that same week Serena enjoyed a visit with all of her girlfriends. Alex's boss, Wyatt, had generously flown Jayne and Molly up from San Diego.

Wyatt. *Hmm.*

More than ever Serena was convinced that something was up between the hunky, hard-edged resort owner and Alex, though Alex was tight-lipped about whatever it was. Something seemed different about Molly, too, although Serena couldn't quite put her finger on what. As for Jayne, she seemed to be recovering from her heartache. She still had a long way to go, but at least some of the sadness had left her eyes.

During their time together the four women enjoyed an afternoon of girl talk and shopping—one that thankfully was not marred by the ever-present media.

It helped that Wyatt had sent a limo to collect Serena. She'd certainly enjoyed arriving in style, even if she did have her own car now. At Jonas's insistence they had gone to a dealership outside the city—not wanting to appear to be currying favor. She'd picked out a sexy little red sports number. Two doors. Two seats. Six gears. It was temporary transportation, she reminded herself. Still, she loved it.

She was having the morning from hell when Jeffrey Kefron finally got back to her. The zipper on her favorite pair of jeans had broken along with one of her fingernails, and she'd dribbled grape jelly down the front of her blouse. All of that was forgotten after their brief telephone conversation. The renowned professor and restaurateur liked what he saw.

"You show originality and outright fear-lessness in your blown sugar work," he told her, his words clipped with an accent she couldn't quite place. "But your technique can use some refinement, and your marzipan flowers and fruit need work. With more training and practice they could be much more lifelike."

They made plans for her to visit his kitchen the following week.

"You're a natural, Mrs. Benjamin. I look forward to meeting you in person."

Serena didn't correct him on her name. After thanking him, she hung up and danced around the tidy living room, tossing the pillows as if they were huge pieces of confetti. She wanted to tell someone the news, to share her joy. Jonas was the first person who came to mind. She hugged one pillow to her chest and talked herself out of it. This was the kind of news one shared with a loved one. So she bypassed the urge to phone him at his office and instead called Alex.

"Oh, Serena! I knew it! Just wait. You're going to have your own TV show someday," Alex said.

"I'll settle for my own shop." But the idea of a nationally televised program had Serena grinning. Wouldn't *that* be something? Anything seemed possible at that moment.

"I wish I could take you out to celebrate tonight," Alex was saying. "Unfortunately there's a lot going on at McKendrick's. I'll be here late."

She didn't sound upset by the prospect. Quite the opposite.

After they'd hung up Serena sent text messages to both Jayne and Molly. Then, even though she didn't call Jonas, she went to work in the kitchen. Tonight, she and her husband would eat cake.

Jonas had had a brutal day. He'd spent the morning fighting his way through a maze of loopholes in a client's contract. In the midst of that, Jameson had called again to criticize Serena's wardrobe choices.

"The jeans she wore to Monday's rally in the park were way too casual," he claimed. "Cindy had on a linen suit. Serena needs to project a more professional image."

"I don't know. Those jeans withstood the assault by that golden retriever puppy that got off its leash far better than Cindy's outfit did." Jonas smiled as he recalled how Serena had taken muddy pawprints and a slobbering tongue in stride, while Cindy had looked ready to call the pound.

Jameson was undeterred. "We have dry cleaners for a reason. I've rescheduled your appointment with Terri Kaufman."

Jonas had scotched meetings with the image consultant twice already. To his campaign manager's dismay he did so again. "Cancel it. Serena doesn't need a makeover."

"Jonas—"

"She's perfect just as she is. If anyone needs to change, it's me," he said, before hanging up on his sputtering campaign manager.

Lunchtime found Jonas touring the pediatric wing of one of the city's hospitals. Congressman Benjamin's efforts in Washington had freed up some funds to allow for several projects in his home district, including the installation of some state-of-the-art diagnostic equipment. It was his father's idea for Jonas to cash in on the family tie. Though he didn't like it, an invitation had been issued, and declining would have looked bad—especially since his mother and sister would be there.

Afterward, Jameson steered Jonas to the maternity ward. Before he knew what was happening he was holding a newborn, while a set of proud parents looked on. Camera shutters snapped; flashes blinded.

"When will you and Mrs. Benjamin—I

mean, Ms. Warren—start a family?" a reporter asked during the photo op.

"We just got married. Give us a little time." He laughed, but as held the feather-light infant in the crook of his arm his heart began to pound.

When would he and Serena start a family? Jonas knew the answer. He'd known the answer since agreeing to an annulment. More and more lately he didn't like it. Just as he hadn't wanted to let Serena go the night they met, he couldn't imagine letting her go now.

"I love her." His knees wobbled and he had to sit, teetering backward until he found a chair. The anxious parents snatched back their child, even as a couple of the nurses who were standing nearby sighed.

"That's why he married Ms. Warren," Jameson interjected with a tight laugh. He clapped his hands. "Unfortunately, ladies and gentlemen, Mr. Benjamin has another function to attend this afternoon and he must be going. Thank you again for coming out today."

He hustled a still-staggered Jonas out the door.

"What the hell was that all about?" he yelled. "You looked ready to faint—and with a newborn in your arms, no less."

Jonas had *felt* ready to faint. His head had finally caught up with his heart.

"I love my wife."

"Yeah, that was a good line. I think it went over well." Jameson tugged his goatee. "We should ramp up the romance angle."

Jonas spent the rest of the afternoon thinking about Serena, their marriage and the future. He needed to convince her to change her mind about the deal they'd struck. He debated just coming out and telling her his true feelings, but after everything that had transpired between them he wasn't sure she would believe him.

So he would show her. He took his cue from Jameson, oddly enough. He would ramp up the romance.

Jonas planned to court his wife.

CHAPTER ELEVEN

Music was on when he arrived at the condo just after five o'clock. It was upbeat, offbeat and loud. Jonas enjoyed his first genuine smile of the day, and that was before he pushed open the kitchen door and found Serena. Just one glance had him sighing and a good portion of his tension ebbing away.

She stood at the counter, using a pastry bag to pipe intricate latticework onto the side of a cake that was several rounded layers tall. Even though the decoration wasn't quite finished it was gorgeous, exquisite. And even though his wife was dusted in flour, the front of her Bob Marley tee-shirt stained with varying hues of frosting, so was she.

"Stunning." Jonas forced his gaze to the cake. "What's the occasion?"

"No occasion." She shrugged, but then a

smile broke free. "Okay, maybe a small one. I spoke to Jeffrey Kefron today."

A small one indeed. Jonas grinned in return. "And?"

"He thinks my works shows 'originality' and 'fearlessness'. That's a quote, by the way." She laughed, obviously delighted.

Jonas was delighted for her. "I knew he would."

"Did you, now?"

"The man's not blind."

Serena laughed again, but this time she seemed oddly self-conscious. "Oh, the time!" Her gaze flew to the clock on the stove. "I've been so wrapped up with this cake I didn't make anything for dinner."

"That's all right. I'd rather take you out."

"Yeah?" Her head tilted to one side. Even without earrings, he found the pose provocative.

"We can celebrate."

Her grin unfurled and tugged at his heart. "I like the sound of that."

Jonas had promised Serena a night she would remember. He was off to a stellar start. While she'd scoured her closet for something to wear, settling on an almost sedate black sheath that she'd punched up with a thick red belt and matching heels, he'd been busy. When they met up in the living room a short time later he was freshly shaved and dressed and holding a bouquet of lavender and sweet pea blooms.

"Wow."

"You never had a proper bouquet," he said as he handed her the flowers.

"Thank you." She brought them to her nose, drew in their sweet scent. "But I meant wow as in you look different."

He was wearing a tailored sports coat—nothing terribly surprising about that. But he'd paired the classic piece with blue jeans, comfortable leather loafers and a basic white button-down shirt.

Jonas's tone was innocent, but his smile pure sin when he replied, "I don't know what you mean. I'm wearing a tie."

Yes, he was—the very one Serena had given him just before their first public appearance as husband and wife. It had been more dare than gift at the time. In truth, she'd never expected to see him don it. She set the bouquet aside and stepped closer. Giving in to the need to touch him, she flattened her palms on his chest for a moment, before pretending to fuss with the Windsor knot. The scent of his cologne teased out a sigh.

"So, where are we going, anyway?"

Again the sinful smile emerged, sending her hormones on red alert. "You'll see," he answered evasively.

Serena loved surprises, but when they arrived at the airport a short time later she was officially flummoxed. Jonas had hired a helicopter to take them to their final destination. The *chop-chop* of its blades made conversation difficult during the flight. Not that it mattered. She was pretty much speechless…and having the time of her life.

The pilot set down at an airfield well outside the city limits. Despite the remote location, a shiny black car was waiting for them. A uniformed driver hopped out to open the rear door as soon as they emerged from the aircraft.

"When did you find the time to do all this?"

He shrugged. "I just made a few phone calls."

It was more than that, though, and they both knew it. He was making a real effort to be romantic and spontaneous. It was almost as if he was trying to be the man who'd first swept her off her feet. The thought made her both giddy and scared.

Finally the car pulled up the long curved drive of a country estate that seemed more suited to the antebellum South than the twenty-first century West.

"What *is* this place?" she asked, taking in the massive white columns that braced either side of an expansive porch. A huge light swayed from the overhang.

"You'll see." Jonas rested his hand on the small of her back as they climbed the steps.

"Welcome to the Piedmont," a man in formal attire said the moment they stepped inside.

Serena soon learned that what appeared to be a private residence on a couple of dozen acres in the middle of the desert was in fact an exclusive restaurant. After they were seated at their table, Jonas explained that half a dozen years earlier a chef from Los Angeles had bought the two-story, five-thousand-square-foot home on a whim and, after extensive renovation, turned it into a premier bed and breakfast, renowned for its comfortable rooms, vast selection of wines and array of whimsical deserts.

"Given what we're celebrating, it seemed a perfect fit," he said.

A server came by to take their drinks order. Serena decided on champagne. Jonas ordered

a bottle for them. As they sipped the sparkling wine the golden glow of the sun disappeared over the horizon and the first stars
began to appear. God help her, the evening
was turning out to be every bit as magical as
the night they'd met.

Serena let out a sigh. "This is nice. Thank
you, Jonas."

"You're welcome. You deserve a night
out on the town. We haven't done that
much, have we?"

"We go out all the time," she protested.

"Campaign stuff. I'm talking about just
you and me out for an evening."

"I understand why we haven't."

"You do?"

"The media," she said, pulling a face. "Reporters are everywhere."

He smiled, but didn't confirm her suspi-
cions. Instead he threw her a complete curve-
ball by asking to see the dessert menu when the
server returned for their dinner order. Afterward he grinned at Serena over the top of the
leather-bound selection of confections he held.

"What's that saying? 'Life's short; order
dessert first.'"

She blinked. "You want dessert now?"

"Why not?"

It was something she would do, and in fact had done on several occasions. But *Jonas*? "What's gotten into you?"

"I have a craving for something sweet." His gaze was on her rather than the menu, and the look in his eyes made it hard for Serena to breathe.

"A c-craving?" she managed to whisper.

"Yes. I've had it a while now. Sometimes it keeps me awake at night."

She knew exactly what he meant, so she nodded—and the rest of the world slipped away.

"Do you know what you want?"

Oh, she knew, all right. She nearly blurted out something totally inappropriate before she realized the server was standing there and Jonas's question was in reference to food.

Serena went with a ridiculously rich slice of devil's food cake, layered with raspberry mousse and covered in shaved bits of white and dark chocolate. It was sin on a plate, and so filling she had no room for more than a few bites of the chicken picata that came later. Both left her unsatisfied, though. She was hungry for something else entirely, and it was clear Jonas was too when he suggested they go for a walk after he'd paid for their meal.

Hand in hand they strolled along a walkway that led to a patio where music played and couples danced. Just before they reached it Jonas took her in his arms. He pressed his cheek against hers as they swayed to the rhythm under the soft glow of paper lanterns.

Heat spiraled through her. "Sh-shouldn't we be getting back?"

"Aren't you enjoying yourself?" he asked.

"A little too much," she murmured as his warm breath feathered across her ear.

"I think I know what you mean." He nipped at the soft flesh of her throat, teasing out a moan. Over the roaring in her ears, Serena heard him say, "We could stay."

The offer was reminiscent of the one he'd made the night they met. *He* was much more like the man she'd met that night—the one who'd been willing to take chances and tempt fate. The man who had danced with her to his own music in the moonlight.

Serena swallowed. "Here?"

"In one of the rooms."

"We…we agreed to…" It was difficult to remember what they'd agreed to with him nibbling his way down her neck.

"To a marriage in name only," Jonas supplied. He stopped kissing her and leaned back far enough to see her face in the dim light. "It's up to you. We can go back to the condo or we can spend the night here. Together."

As husband and wife.

Serena knew that was what he was saying—just as she knew what her answer should be. He'd said nothing about changing the length of their marriage, only its current terms.

Even so, she brought her mouth to his. A wanton kiss served as her reply.

Jonas's heart was pounding like a jack-hammer by the time he and Serena reached the second-floor bedroom he'd booked along with the reservation for dinner, hoping the evening would turn out just as it had.

He closed the door behind them, trying to keep his breathing slow and even. As desperate as he felt, he was determined to pace himself. His resolve was tested the moment Serena slipped off her shoes. As he watched, she rubbed the back of one calf with the opposite foot and then settled on the edge of the mattress.

"What are you doing way over there?" she asked.

"Trying to remember how to be a gentleman." And failing miserably. In his mind he was peeling off her dress, and whatever lacy bits were beneath it.

She reached behind her back to slide down the zipper on her dress. The smile she sent him all but stopped his heart. "You know, a real gentleman would offer his assistance."

The outside world fell away with their clothes. Stress and frustration dissipated with each moan and sigh. What remained left Jonas humbled, and feeling incredibly lucky.

After the storm of their lovemaking had ebbed they lay together, legs and arms tangled with the sheets.

She huffed out a breath. "Wow. That was better than I remembered. And I have a pretty good memory."

Jonas chuckled. "Agreed. It *was* pretty damned good."

"Understatement." She offered her pet phrase.

"Great?" he allowed with a smile.

"Understatement," she said again, and flopped onto her back. The pose left her breasts exposed.

Jonas felt his blood begin to heat again. He managed in a nonchalant tone, "You're just fishing for compliments."

"That implies I'm exaggerating." The

corners of her mouth tugged up. Her gaze held a dare. "Am I?"

"No. I don't think so."

Her eyes closed. Her smile turned decidedly carnal. "You don't *think* so."

"Hard to say," he murmured.

"What will it take to convince you?" She punctuated the question with a caress that left him speechless. "Mmm. I thought so," Serena all but purred as she rolled atop him.

As he had been since he'd first met her, Jonas found himself lost.

Serena was humming when she hung up the telephone the next day. She'd called Alex, seeking some advice on how to proceed with Jonas, but they'd never gotten around to the subject after her friend had dropped the bombshell that she was getting married.

Married!

Serena's intuition that Wyatt McKendrick was much more to her friend than a boss had been right. Apparently Wyatt was no longer the distant, driven man who had first offered Alex a job. And it was clear her friend was besotted. She was happy for them. After last night she wanted to be believe she and Jonas had a chance at happily-ever-after, too. But he'd said nothing about love, nothing about wanting to stay married for keeps. She'd kept her feelings to herself, afraid to express what was in her heart. It was so fragile and foreign. She'd never felt so vulnerable.

Jameson stopped by the condo unexpectedly a little later.

"Jonas isn't here," she told him. "He had to meet a client outside the city. He probably won't be home for another hour or so."

"That explains why he's been so hard to reach today."

"Is something wrong?"

"No. Quite the contrary. I came to congratulate him and discuss how we capitalize on this." For the first time in their acquaintance Jameson smiled warmly at her. "The PR stunt the two of you pulled last night was brilliant. It's on the front page of today's *Sun*."

"I'm afraid I'm not following you."

"Yesterday's jaunt to the Piedmont. The media are lapping it up, and so are the voters." Jameson came inside and set his briefcase on the foyer table so he could open it. He pulled out a folded section of newspaper and handed it to her. "This is the kind of publicity we can really use right now."

"Lovebirds finally enjoy a honeymoon"

was the headline. She couldn't bring herself to read the copy beneath it. Besides, there was no need. The picture of her and Jonas dancing in the moonlight on the lighted walk outside the Piedmont was worth a thousand words. Serena didn't like what they were saying.

"This was…planned?"

"You know Jonas. He never does anything without a good reason."

"Except marry me."

Jameson seemed to take delight in replying. "Yes, but he's making the most of it. Just yesterday afternoon I told him we should punch up the romance angle."

Well, he'd certainly listened. Serena recalled their lovemaking the evening before and her stomach roiled. No wonder Jonas hadn't said anything about falling in love or wanting to forgo an annulment. Neither was his intention. That didn't make him a liar. What it made her, was a fool. A chill swept over her along with a truth she didn't want to accept. She handed the newspaper back to Jameson.

"Is that all you came by to say?" she asked, proud of herself for sounding so normal when inside she was dying.

"Yes." But Jameson hesitated. "Actually, now that I'm here, I have a favor to ask."

Red flags waved, but she was too broken to care. "What might that be?"

"I've made an appointment for you to meet with a personal stylist about your image. Jonas has canceled it twice. I think he's worried about offending you—especially since you've been such a good sport in all of this."

"That's me. A good sport."

Jameson continued. "The most recent poll of likely voters shows Jonas trailing Davenport by two percentage points. Given the margin of error, that might be nothing, but I think we need to hedge our bets. Davenport does well with older voters, and they tend to be the most reliable about going to the polls on Election Day, so they're who we need to target.

"Before Jonas married you he was slightly ahead in the same poll. Part of that could be attributed to the former Mayor's endorsement of him, but not all. He was seen as a wildcard by some, but not for the same reasons he's considered a wildcard now. His marriage—coming out of the blue as it did—has some people concerned about his temperament."

His gaze was pointed.

"You don't like me, do you?" she asked.

"My job is neither to like nor to dislike

you. My job is to mitigate the effect you're having on my candidate's bid for office."

"A minute ago you were pleased with my effect," she reminded him.

"No. I was happy with how Jonas was able to use it. It could still backfire—especially if the media ever get wind of how brief your acquaintance was before you exchanged vows. Do you want to help him or not?"

What *she* wanted was of little consequence here. Helping Jonas get elected was why she had come back to Vegas, even if she'd begun to kid herself that another reason might exist. Serena picked up the pieces of her shattered heart and worked up a smile worthy of an Oscar-winning actress. "Good sport that I am, I'm always willing to do what I can for the team."

Jameson nodded his approval before taking the image consultant's card from his briefcase and handing it to Serena. His smile was triumphant. "She'll be expecting your call."

The drive back to the city took forever—especially since Jonas was so eager to see Serena. They hadn't spoken since that morning, and then only briefly. After they'd returned from the Piedmont he'd only had time to shave and change into fresh clothes before hurrying off for his appointment. At that time they'd agreed to a quiet evening in. She'd promised to make dinner, and something decadent for dessert. He had something decadent in mind, too.

When he arrived home she was standing in the foyer, not waiting to greet him, but holding her purse and slipping her feet into a pair of pointed flats.

"Are you going out?"

"I've got an appointment with Terri Kaufman at four-thirty."

Her posture was rigid, her tone cool and detached. Still, he was sure he must have heard her wrong. "The image consultant?" he asked.

"Yes. Given the urgency of the situation, she agreed to shuffle her schedule so she could see me this afternoon."

Jonas gaped at Serena in confusion. "What urgency?"

"The most recent poll numbers. They show Roderick has a slight lead."

"Very slight—as in it's too close to call."

"All the more reason to be proactive," she replied matter-of-factly. "We need to target those older voters who might be put off by a woman who would wear white after Labor Day."

"You sound like Jameson. What's going on?"

"I decided I need to do a better job holding up my end of our deal since you've gone to so much trouble."

She was angry and upset. That much came through loud and clear in her icy stare and clipped tone. But why? He didn't have to wait long to find out. She grabbed the copy of the *Sun* from the foyer table and handed it to him.

The photograph of the two of them ran three columns wide on the front page. This must be what Jameson had called about earlier, Jonas realized. His campaign manager had left messages at Jonas's office and on his cellphone, pleased as punch about some positive news coverage. Jonas had assumed he'd been referring to the photo op at the hospital. But this was Jonas and Serena, wrapped in a steamy embrace. It was a precious and private moment that had been caught by a camera and now released to the masses.

As a political candidate, as well as the son of a veteran politician, Jonas was used to seeing his image splashed in the newspaper. It went with the territory. Privacy while out in public was never guaranteed. Still, it bothered him that he hadn't realized someone was hiding nearby with a camera while he'd danced with his wife.

He viewed it with a critical eye. At least it was a decent shot of both of them—especially Serena, since she more fully faced the camera. She appeared lovely and happy. Her expression was soft, open. And the way she was looking at him...

"You're beautiful," he said softly. "This is a hazard of public life, I'm afraid. But at least they captured you perfectly."

"That's not my best side," she disagreed, before adding, "You should have told me where to look. I could have put on a better show."

He frowned. "What do you mean by that? Do you think I had something to do with this?"

She merely raised her brows.

"I went to a lot of trouble to avoid this," he reminded her. "I wanted to be with you alone, away from here."

"I thought you wanted to celebrate the call I got from Jeffrey Kefron?"

"That too. All of that." He waved his arms, feeling both impatient and desperate.

"You went to a lot of trouble and

expense. But then PR such as this is priceless. The Davenport camp must be green with envy."

"What's gotten into you? When I saw you this morning everything between us was fine. We were…happy. Now you're flinging accusations and acting as if the only thing between us is that damned deal."

Her cool snapped then. "That's because 'that damned deal' *is* the only thing between us!"

"Last night—"

She shook a finger in his face. Her eyes were bright with more than anger. "Don't talk about last night. Don't you dare bring it up right now or I swear…I swear…"

The ground seemed to shift beneath him. Jonas struggled to find his footing. "You're upset right now. I don't know why, or about what, but it has you saying things that aren't true. I think we need to sit down and discuss this."

She squeezed her eyes shut. "Just answer one question for me."

"Anything."

"Did Jameson suggest stoking up the romance angle for your campaign's sake yesterday afternoon?"

"Serena—"

"Yes or no? Just answer the question, dammit!"

"Yes, but—"

She was out the door before he could finish. For a second time that one very small word had dictated Jonas's fate.

CHAPTER TWELVE

THE meeting with Terri Kaufman had taken less than an hour, but Serena didn't return to the condo until after ten. She'd driven out to the desert afterward, where she'd watched the sun set and tried to figure out what she was going to do next.

She didn't have a clue.

Unlike Terri, who'd been full of ideas for how to tone down Serena's eclectic style while still keeping a young and fresh look. Sitting in her car, she leafed through a couple of the catalogs the woman had given her. Terri had helpfully circled the best choices: A-line skirts that skimmed the knee and structured jackets dominated her new fashion-do list. As far as Serena could see the color palate was the only nod to "young and fresh," and even then there was a catch. The handful of bright hues and funky prints allowed in her wardrobe would be relegated to accent pieces such as handbags and scarves.

Terri had also suggested Serena dye her hair a less rich shade of auburn. It would photograph better, she claimed. And a headband might work to keep it back from her face on those occasions when she chose to wear it down, which Terri felt shouldn't be often. When it was all said and done Serena would be a clone of Janet, minus the blonde hair and blue eyes.

Should she follow through on this? Could she? For that matter, could she see the bargain she'd made with Jonas through to the end, knowing what she knew now? With more questions than answers, she flipped closed the catalog and headed back to the city. Never had she felt more miserable and lost.

Jonas wasn't in the living room when she got home, but the sliver of light coming from under his door told her he was still awake. It was cowardly, but she decided to slip into her bedroom undetected. She felt too raw to face him right now. But he opened his door just as she turned to close hers. He was wearing a pair of cotton drawstring pants and a plain white tee-shirt that pulled tight across the very chest she'd woken splayed over this morning. Had it really been mere hours since the future had seemed so full of possibilities?

"You're back. I was getting a little worried."

"Sorry."

He leaned against the doorjamb. "So, how'd the appointment go?"

"Okay. We have another one in two days. That's when the real work will begin, according to Terri. In the meantime, she gave me a lot of suggestions to consider."

"You don't have to take them, Serena."

She lifted her shoulders with a negligence she didn't feel. "It's just clothes and accessories. Well, and hair, too. You'll find this amusing. She wants me to dye it."

Jonas wasn't amused. He looked appalled as he pushed away from the jamb. "No! Serena—"

"Oh, don't worry. Nothing crazy. Actually, she wants me to tone down the color right along with the rest of me." She managed a laugh. "No surprise there, right?"

"Don't dye your hair. Don't change anything. I like you the way you are."

"Why?" At his baffled expression she added, "God knows, I'm no Janet Kinkaid."

"Janet? What the hell does she have to do with this?"

"I met her, Jonas. She came here the day we were having dinner with your parents."

"You never mentioned it."

"My bad." She shrugged.

"Janet and I were over a long time ago."

"Apparently she didn't get that memo. She had a message for you." Serena swallowed. "She said to tell you she'd be there once I was out of the picture."

"I don't want Janet. Nor do I want you out of the picture."

Though a part of her busted-up heart thrilled upon hearing his words, Serena argued, "But she's so perfect. She fits into your life and lifestyle so much better than I do. She'd be a real asset to you, politically and otherwise."

"You don't give yourself enough credit."

"Yes, well, at least you wouldn't have to manufacture a romantic interlude to try and score points with voters."

Anger flashed on his face. "That's not what I did."

"You admitted that Jameson said you should focus on our romance around the media."

"Jameson said that, yes. But it wasn't my motive for taking you to the Piedmont last night, and it sure as hell wasn't why I wanted to stay with you. Nor did I know we were being photographed while we were outside and that a story was going to run in today's paper."

She wanted to believe him, but she wasn't sure what was real anymore, and she felt too vulnerable to put her heart on the line. She'd been playing a role for weeks, putting on a good show for voters and the media. She slipped into that role now for Jonas.

"I think we should go back to just being roommates and concentrate on your election."

"And when the election is over?"

She took a deep breath. "We'll get an annulment, just as we planned."

"Is that really what you want?"

Serena steeled her heart against his wounded expression. It was better this way, she told herself. Better for both of them. "I'm not good at the long term, Jonas. Things between us will end eventually anyway."

"You're sure of that?"

"Aren't you? We're too different. You dated Janet for five years before you claim you figured out she was wrong for you. We've barely known one another for five weeks. I'm just trying to save us both the hassle."

"The heartache, you mean."

She pressed her lips together and said nothing as she backed into her room and closed the door.

Jonas lay awake the better part of the night. Serena was wrong about them—wrong about herself. He'd thought her fearless. It turned out she was scared and more vulnerable than he'd ever imagined. He was scared, too. And no wonder. Love…commitment. Despite the fact they were married, this was uncharted territory for both of them. Jonas was certain of one thing, though, and he became more certain of it with each passing hour: he didn't want Serena for a roommate. He wasn't looking for someone to share his home for the interim. He wanted someone to share his life forever. And that someone was Serena.

Now he had to convince her of that, and he had far less time to do it than he'd thought originally. No more layering. No more foundation-building. She was the sort of woman who would require more than a declaration of love. What he needed was an over-the-top gesture to convince her. He just had to figure out what that was.

* * *

Serena did her best to avoid Jonas in the days that followed. It was relatively easy since she made herself scarce whenever he was home. She had a second appointment with Terri Kaufman. Clothes were bought. Fittings ensued. Alterations were made. Serena drew the line at having her hair colored. Dammit, she liked her natural red. But she acquiesced when it came to its style. She learned how to blow it out straight and create a sleek French twist. She also now owned half a dozen head-bands. She still wasn't sure she could bring herself to wear them out in public, or any of the outfits they went with, for that matter.

More enjoyable by far was her meeting with Jeffrey Kefron. She felt utterly free to express her true self while in his kitchen. When he asked her to sketch out a design for a specialty cake, she allowed her imagination free rein and was rewarded with his praise.

"But the real test will be in the execution," Jeffrey reminded her as they made plans to meet again. "Following through on what your vision is is the hard part."

His words could apply to another aspect of her life, she thought as she got into her car. Instead of driving home she headed to McKendrick's, in need of a sounding board.

Despite the late hour, Alex was in her office. When Serena arrived they called Jayne and Molly, and Serena confided the events of the past week. She left nothing out. The time for spin—political or otherwise—was past.

"We're basically co-existing right now," she admitted on a watery sigh. "God, we might as well be my parents."

"You're nothing like your parents," Jayne assured her. "You're not actively seeking to make one another miserable."

Serena snorted. "Maybe not, but we're doing a damned good job of it."

"It sounds to me like the two of you are in love," Alex said.

"That's only because you're about to be married and have love on the brain."

"No. You're in love." This from Molly. "You fell for him the first night you met. Sometimes and for some people it happens that fast. It's time to own up, Serena."

"I…" She raised her shoulders in a shrug that only Alex could see. After a moment she said quietly, "He's never said he loves me."

"How many times have *you* said it?" Jayne wanted to know.

"I…haven't."

"What are you waiting for?" Alex asked.

"I don't know. A sign, I guess. Proof positive that I'm not setting myself up for disaster."

"That's not the way love works," Alex said softly.

"You have to put yourself out there," Molly added.

Jayne's response was born of painful experience. "You have to be willing to risk everything."

Serena's eyes filled. "I feel like I already have."

Alex reached over to squeeze her hand. "Sorry, honey. But if you haven't told Jonas your true feelings you haven't come close."

The new furniture Serena had ordered for the condo arrived. She spent half a day arranging it, hanging the curtains and setting out the accessories she'd bought during happier times. How ironic, she thought, eyeing her handiwork when she finished. The apartment now reflected her personality far more than her new wardrobe did.

Saturday arrived. The weekends were hard, since both of them were home during the day. This one was especially nerve-racking. She and Jonas were to be the guests of honor at a Concerned Pastors of Las

Vegas luncheon. Campaign donations were on the line, or so Serena had overheard Jameson tell Jonas. And she would be test-driving her new look.

She spent half an hour blowing out her hair and straightening it with a flat iron. The sleek style looked pretty good on her until she topped it off with an ivory grosgrain headband. She pulled a face at her reflection in the mirror before going to dress. The ivory sheath with navy piping was classic and demure. It had a square neckline and cap sleeves. She'd fit in at the country club now for sure.

"God, what am I doing?" she asked her reflection.

She sank onto the side of the bed. She couldn't twist herself into a Stepford Wife—not even for Jonas. Especially since he didn't appear to want her to in the first place. She'd hoped to hide behind the clothes, she realized. Play a role and pretend none of this mattered to her. But it did.

"Serena, we've got to go," Jonas called from the hall. "We're already running late."

Even so, it took her several more minutes to regain her composure. Then, pulling off the headband, she headed for the living room. Jonas turned when she entered. He had on a suit and tie. Interestingly, both the suit's cut and the tie's print were more edgy than he usually wore. But it was her transformation that took center stage. His mouth went slack.

"I…I can't do this."

He exhaled in relief. "Thank God! No offense. You look lovely. But I like you better as, well, *you*."

The compliment was like balm on blistered skin. Serena swallowed. *Tell him you love him. Risk it all.* Her friends had said. She hadn't realized she was such a coward until the declaration caught in her throat. The words that made it out were, "That's not what I mean. I can't do *this* anymore. I want to exercise the easy get-out clause we agreed to."

He stepped toward her, arms outstretched. "Serena, please—"

She backed away. "You…you can tell people I had to return to San Diego to take care of an ailing relative. Jameson can spin it, I'm sure."

"Let's talk about this. I have things I want to say—things I need to tell you."

"Okay, but later." She attempted a smile. "You have a luncheon to attend. You don't want to be late."

"You're not going with me?"

"No. I can't go dressed like this, and dressed like myself I won't do you any good." Though it pained her to say it, she added, "You'll be fine without me."

He debated his options before sighing. "Promise you'll be here when I get back?"

Serena nodded. "I'll be here."

She would be there, but by the time Jonas returned she planned to have packed her suitcases and booked a flight to San Diego. The only thing that would be left to say would be goodbye.

The last place Jonas wanted to be at that moment was a fund-raising luncheon where he was expected to smile and work the crowd. Unfortunately he had little choice, but as soon as possible he would make his excuses and head for the exit—consequences be damned.

"Where's Serena?" Jameson asked, glancing around. "I'm eager to see Terri Kaufman's work in the flesh."

"She won't be here."

"Is she sick?"

"More like fed up," Jonas muttered. And he didn't blame her.

Jameson let the comment pass. "Maybe that's just as well. I wanted to warn you that

Colleen Daring, the host of that cable program *Vegas 24/7*, is here. The media weren't supposed to be invited, but apparently she's close friends with the wife of Reverend Saunders. She brought a cameraman, and when I spoke to her earlier her smile could have drawn blood. She's eager to make a name for herself. Steer clear of her if you can."

Jonas managed to do so until just prior to lunch. Colleen ambushed him as he stood outside the banquet room trying to reach Serena on his cell. No one was picking up at the condo. When he turned, the keen-eyed reporter was hot-footing it toward him. She had a microphone in one hand and was motioning for her cameraman to catch up with her.

"Mr. Benjamin, a moment of your time, please?"

"Sorry. I'm not here to give interviews. I'm just a guest of the Concerned Pastors today."

"And no doubt eager for its membership's donations."

He ignored the comment. "I have to get back inside. If you want to schedule an interview, you'll have to contact my staff."

"Five minutes. That's all I need."

He smiled politely, but started toward the door.

"I understand from a reliable source that

you met your wife in a hotel lounge on the Strip and wed her the very same night," she called after him.

Jonas swiveled back. Briefly he considered offering Jameson's fabricated tale of how he and Serena were lovers reunited. Instead he nodded. "That's right."

The bald admission took her by surprise. "You knew a woman for mere hours and you married her?"

"You've seen my wife, Ms. Daring. Can you blame me?"

The reporter's smile turned cunning. "Are you trying to tell me that the man who would be Las Vegas's next mayor fell victim to its oldest cliché?"

"You think love is a cliché?"

"Not at all." But then she shot back, "Are you saying it was love at first sight?"

"I am." Jonas shook his head in dismay. "But, like you, I doubted it. That kind of thing doesn't happen, right? Not to people as shrewd or pragmatic as we are."

The reporter nodded, but a line formed between her brows as she waited for him to go on.

"Do you know what's really funny, though? And by funny I don't mean humorous. More like painfully ironic. By the time I figured out that my first instinct was right, I'd blown it."

"What do you mean?"

"My wife is leaving me, Ms. Daring. She wants to go back to San Diego, and for good reason. When I asked Serena to come back to Vegas after our wedding I didn't offer her a real marriage. I was more interested in saving my political hide. Or at least that's what I'd convinced myself. I couldn't admit I loved her. I couldn't admit it to her or even to myself. Now that I can, it may be too late."

Colleen lowered the microphone. "This isn't all for show, is it? You really mean it."

"I mean it." Jonas sighed. "There—you have your story, and it's an exclusive. Be kind in the editing."

He started to walk away, but she called him back. "It's an exclusive, all right, but I don't get the feeling it's completely accurate."

"It's the truth, I assure you. Every word."

"A good reporter relies on more than one source." Her smile was calculating. "Are you interested in trying to save your marriage?"

"What do you have in mind?"

CHAPTER THIRTEEN

SERENA hung up the telephone and replayed the odd conversation she'd just had with Jonas. The luncheon was over, but he wasn't coming home. Instead he had an interview to do—a live one on a local cable news program. This time he hadn't made her promise she would remain at the condo until he returned. No, he'd merely asked her to tune in to the show.

Serena finished packing her bags. The earliest flight on which there was an available seat didn't leave till the morning, so she'd called Alex. A room was waiting at McKendrick's. It was time to go. As she passed through the living room on her way to the door, she hesitated. Jonas's interview would be starting. Curiosity got the better of her. She hunted down the remote and switched on the TV.

"Good afternoon, Las Vegas," a dark-haired, sharp-featured woman announced. She was seated at a desk, with a panoramic rendering of the Strip featured in the faux window behind her. "I'm Colleen Daring, and this is *Las Vegas 24/7*, where we bring you Sin City's news when it happens, whatever the hour. The news today concerns mayoral hopeful Jonas Benjamin. "Welcome to the show, Mr. Benjamin."

The camera panned to the host's left, where Jonas sat in a red club chair, looking oddly nervous and impossibly handsome.

"Thanks for having me."

"Let's get right down to business, shall we? I ran into you earlier today and asked you some very pointed questions about your marriage."

Serena sucked in a breath. Jonas, however, appeared more relaxed as he answered, "That's right. You weren't expecting me to be quite so honest, were you?"

Colleen chuckled. "No. I have to admit I wasn't." She transferred her gaze to the camera. "I asked Mr. Benjamin to confirm a rumor I'd heard that he'd married his wife mere hours after meeting her in a lounge."

Serena gasped. This was the political nightmare they'd done their best to avoid.

But Jonas didn't appear the least bit concerned. In fact, he grinned. "You didn't call it a rumor, Ms. Daring. I believe you claimed to have heard it from a very reliable source."

The woman shrugged. "For the benefit of viewers, will you tell them what you told me?"

"Serena and I first met in a hotel lounge in June. She was in town with friends. I saw her and…" He shook his head in bemusement. "I can't explain what happened when I saw her. I just knew I had to meet her. And then, a handful of hours later, I knew I had to marry her."

Colleen aimed a finger at the camera. "I have to admit I thought his response a bunch of tripe when I heard it. Or, worse, that his campaign was trying to exploit his marriage to improve Mr. Benjamin's chances of election. But a man trying to get elected doesn't say *this*. Roll tape."

Serena sucked in a breath as she watched the footage.

"My wife is leaving me, Ms. Daring. She wants to go back to San Diego, and for good reason. When I asked Serena to come back to Vegas after our wedding I didn't offer her a real marriage. I was more interested in saving my political hide. Or at least that's what I'd convinced myself. I couldn't admit I loved her. I couldn't admit it to her or even to myself. Now that I can, it may be too late."

"For the record, let me ask that again," Colleen said when the camera cut back to her. "Do you love your wife?"

"I have only one word to answer that. It's a word my wife uses often." He smiled into the camera. "Understatement."

Serena was crying before he'd finished. Jonas loved her. He'd admitted as much on television, and not for the sake of his campaign. Of that she was sure, since he hadn't sugarcoated the origins of their relationship.

Colleen Daring was back on. "Now, viewers know me. I'm not the warm and fuzzy type. When Mr. Benjamin said what you just heard him say—well, my reporter instincts kicked in. He's risking his campaign for this woman. He also claims he's risking his heart. So, I have to know. What's Serena Warren's side of the story? Where does she stand? As always, I believe in a balanced report." The woman grinned then. "You've got thirty minutes to get to the studio, Ms. Warren."

Serena shut off the television and shot to her feet. Her cellphone was ringing before she hit the foyer. Alex.

"Can't talk," she hollered into it. "I'm on my way out the door."

"You'd better be hustling to the TV station."

She slowed her stride, but didn't stop. "You saw it?"

"Wyatt's a fan. He called me in when Jonas came on. Do you know where the place is located?"

"Not exactly."

"Wyatt said it's close enough for you to walk."

"Good. But I plan to run. I'm putting myself out there, Alex."

"That a girl," her friend said, before giving directions.

The studio wasn't as impressive-looking in reality as it was on the TV. Serena didn't care. What mattered was that Jonas was there and he loved her. What was more, she'd finally found the courage to tell him she loved him, too.

Someone from make-up doused her in a cloud of powder before she hit the set. Jonas was no longer sitting in one of the club chairs. Before she could ask where he was, she was wired for a microphone and introduced to Colleen.

"And we're live," a man in the studio called as a red light flicked on.

"Hello, Las Vegas. I'm Colleen Daring, back with Serena Warren, wife of mayoral candidate Jonas Benjamin." The host smiled at Serena. "We barely had a chance to meet before going live. I want to thank you for hustling down here. From your timeliness, I take it you were watching the segment?"

"Yes. Jonas called and asked me to."

"So you saw the clip I shot earlier today?"

"I did."

"Were you surprised?" the woman asked.

Serena nodded as her hands knotted painfully in her lap. "But I shouldn't have been."

"Why do you say that?"

"I should have trusted Jonas. I didn't. Not because of anything he'd done. But because I was scared."

"Do you love him?"

Serena glanced around the set. She didn't see her husband anywhere.

"Ms. Warren? Are you going to answer the question?"

"Only if the right person asks it."

Colleen Daring smiled. "I think I know just who you mean."

A moment later Jonas finally appeared on

the set. He looked so gorgeous and welcoming that Serena had to resist the urge to leap into his arms.

"Ms. Warren says she wants you to ask the question," Colleen said, for benefit of the camera.

"I have a question for her, but it's not the one that you just asked." He grinned. "I figured out the answer to that one a while ago, and it was confirmed the moment she showed up here."

"So what do you want to ask her?" The host seemed genuinely baffled.

Serena was, too. Until Jonas stepped in front of her and went down on one knee. He held out a ring—a big black opal that was shot full of vibrant colors. It wasn't a traditional engagement ring, which made it the perfect choice for Serena.

"I got it right when I asked you to be my wife. I've screwed up plenty since then, but I'm asking you now, here in front of Ms. Daring and whatever potential voters may be watching, if you, Serena Jean Warren, will stay married to me? I love you, Serena. I want to love you for a lifetime."

She was crying before he got through his proposal. "Yes," she managed between sniffles. "I want to stay married to you. I love you, too, Jonas. I'm sorry it took me so long to say it."

He slipped the ring on her finger and rose to kiss her.

Long after the show cut to commercial they were still kissing.